Their Deadly Game

Anna Ioannidi

Published by Anna Ioannidi, 2024.

THEIR DEADLY GAME

First edition. August 25, 2024.

Copyright © 2024 Anna Ioannidi.

ISBN: 979-8227410900

Written by Anna Ioannidi.

To all the good girls who would love to be chased by three serial killers in a maze. This one is for you.

Trigger Warning

Please read this list before you continue. This book contains sensitive subjects! Your mental health matters.

Stay safe & happy reading!

- Child abuse
- Alcoholism
- Child birth mention
- Death of a child
- Death of a parent
- Death of a family member
- Death of a Sibling
- Arson
- Abandonment
- Mention of Foster care system
- Mention of Domestic Abuse
- Adoption
- Mention of Teen Pregnancy
- Mention of SA of a minor
- Car accident
- Captivity & confinement
- Explicit language

Liam

"**G**et her."

Nate's voice echoes into the night, as he speeds up chasing the woman through the dark maze.

She is trying to escape us, running through that maze like her life depends on it. *And it does.*

"Keep running, little slut."

Mike taunts from behind me and I laugh watching the poor woman fall to the ground.

She quickly gets back up and runs again, she is searching for the scarecrow, that little glimpse of freedom.

The rules of our twisted little game are simple: If she gets to the scarecrow we will spare her life. In addition to this, if she remains hidden until the sun rises, she may try another night.

Of course, the rules don't really matter, and none of the women who have played our game got out alive. It is the false sense of hope that makes them fight, and that is the only part all three of us love.

Watching them fight for their lives, running and screaming, trying to figure out a way to remain hidden or to locate a scarecrow in the middle of a hay maze they have never stepped foot before. This alone can make my night. They get so desperate that their screams fill the night along with the sound of our engines.

A deadly game under our rules. Some of them almost get close to the scarecrow, some almost remain hidden for the entirety of the night. Others give up from the start, those I don't like. You can see them give up from the moment they start running. They know their fate, and I can't keep myself from wondering how someone ends up in a life and death situation and doesn't fight.

I am not a therapist, but I am pretty sure those are the ones that are already broken. There are two types of people in this world surviving trauma. You have the ones that come out of it as fighters. They will sell their souls to survive, burn the world to the ground, and roast marshmallows while they watch everything become ash. Then, you have the ones that give up and accept fate.

Mike and I always belonged in the first category, sometimes more literally than others. We burned my house to the ground once with my father inside. Sadly, some innocent lives were lost in the process. But the dick that liked to slice our backs with his belt went down with them. That's the only reason I don't regret it.

Maybe that's why we started playing this game, the need to cause the pain we received. A twisted way to cope. Mike needs it more than myself, he is the one who started it all. He suffered through so much horror that this is the only way he copes. Through blood and screams. Violence calms his inner demons. It feeds the monster he has become.

I am fully aware that this is a twisted sense of fun we have. I am sure an actual psychiatrist would have a field day trying to figure out how our psychotic brains work.

I speed up and circle the woman who is now more scared than ever, but I am not the one she should be afraid of, I have never once been the one to kill any of them. I find nothing in the kills. Their blood is not what I want. Their screams though, that's something else. The chase is what excites me, the part of taking a life has never been my thing.

My cousin is another case entirely, he loves the bloodshed. He lives for the kills and the adrenaline that comes from it.

"Hello, little one"

He coos at her smiling.

He has ditched his bike and now is on foot with a knife in one hand and a twisted smile on his face. He is fucking crazy and I love him to death, but this side of him even scares me. His eyes have a spark, they only get when he holds a knife or a gun on someone. It is like their fear works like a drug for him.

"Did you really think you could escape us?" Nate taunts from his side, his bike missing too.

I get off mine and join them. Nate has always been calmer, and more calculated. He has been the one that seems to enjoy the hunts the least, but if I had to guess I would say he is the one getting horny by them.

The fact, that he is fucking Mike, every time we finish one is what proves my suspicion. Those two are like a weird old couple that uses murder as an aphrodisiac.

This woman seems to have a plan, she is looking around with a purpose. It looks like she is calculating something, searching for the scarecrow. She looks like she knows the maze better than the rest, but I wouldn't bet any money on her finding it.

She is running clearly, following a path she only knows exists. I am pretty sure she is confident in herself, that she will survive this. Delusional in every sense of the word, if you ask me.

Suddenly, she stops. She has made it to the scarecrow.

We close in on her, and she turns to me and declares,

"I reached the scarecrow!"

I laugh and look at Nate. She turns her gaze to him and repeats.

"That was your stupid rule. I reached it. I am safe!"

She is now angry, and with a good reason.

"Looks like you indeed made it to the scarecrow."

Nate points out with a cold voice.

The woman thinks she has found a friend among us. He sure will let her live. He is the one calling the shots, or at least it seems like he does.

We know, though, that he is not the one in charge. We all have our roles. But Mike is the one making the rules of the game. The one that needs it more than all three of us.

"Time's up bitch."

Mike taunts as a gunshot echoes through the night.

The woman's lifeless body falls on the hay and the night is silent again.

Told you, Nate isn't the one calling the shots. His crazy boyfriend is. Blood spills from her body, and the hay turns a pretty maroon color. I stand in front of her observing the blood, as it tints the spot she has fallen on.

"That was a fun night."

Mike says with excitement, and I ignore him.

There is a sense of guilt, that washes over me after the hunt is done. Fragments of sadness after taking a life. We are playing with fire. Taking lives, like some psychotic gods.

I lift her lifeless body and place it over my motorcycle.

Nate approaches slowly from behind.

"We are going for food and then back to the house."

He lets me know.

Even though their routine is always the same. Hunt - Eat - Fuck - Sleep. Mike is already reaching the edge of the maze and Nate gets on his motorcycle to follow him, as I take the dead woman on her final journey. *Time to go, little one. I am sorry this was your ending.* I say the words inside my head.

I drive to the edge of the maze, where the two men are waiting for me before we part ways. We have always made sure we leave at the same time and separate on the road.

It will make it easier to flee if we are all three at the crime scene, in the rare case we get caught. It hasn't happened so far, maybe it never will, but I doubt that.

I make sure to plan every detail. That has always been my role in this. Making sure we will remain free, no matter what. I must be doing a good job, since we are still walking around killing women like nothing.

I reach the edge, where the white van we use to kidnap the women and transport them to the maze is.

I put the woman in the plastic, we have in the back of the van for that reason. Essentially a body bag. Quickly zip her up, closing her eyes before I do. *Rest in peace sweetie.*

I add my motorcycle next to her and secure it with the chains we have installed there.

"Ready!" I announce.

The boys rev their engines in response. I get in the driver's seat, and I see them leave following close behind, until we get to the crossroad.

They continue straight ahead, taking the road that leads back to the town, and I take a left turn to get on the highway. The trip to the next town is about three hours.

Enough time to calm down from the adrenaline of the hunt, a crucial thing for the next step. I need to be on top of my senses for the task at hand.

Disposing of her body. That's what is next, while the boys do their ritual of sex and food, I am in charge of getting rid of the evidence.

Getting rid of her body is, what I need to do first, returning to her house and making sure we didn't leave a mess when we took her is the next. The last step is something, I am glad to skip today. We had enough time to check, before we left the location of her house, when we kidnapped her.

Her house is on an empty road, the last one, up to a hill, and the next neighbor is at least five minutes distance from it.

She lived there alone and it will take months before anyone even notices she is missing, I can't keep myself from feeling sad for her. In a twisted way, judging the way her life was, we might have done her a favor.

Ending her life doesn't seem like the worst thing that happened to her, but at the same time, I admire the way she fought, even if there was nothing worth fighting for in her life.

Liam

I have been driving for an hour already, the first drops of rain started about thirty minutes ago, and now it is pouring like crazy.

It will make things a little difficult, but it will also help hide my tracks, and that is something I always welcome.

The sound of rain is something that calms me down, like almost washing my sins. It is a little harder to wash them, when they hit the side of your car with every turn. The sound coming from the back reminds me, I have a dead body in a bag there.

I should have strapped her down, with the chains we use for the bikes or something. I wasn't expecting the road to be so slippery. I have been close to losing control of the car a couple of times already.

Suddenly, the sound of a siren breaks through the sound of rain, and I freeze. I can't do anything else than stop, when I see from the rear-view mirror the officer's signal. *Okay calm down Liam, this is not your first rodeo.*

I pick up my phone. I write: **I am getting milk** and hit send. It's our code, in case we get stopped by a police car or being questioned for any reason. A simple enough message that won't raise suspicion in the wrong hands. I sent it to Nate, he is going to be ready to call the lawyers if needed.

I quickly zip my Jacket, making sure no blood stains are visible. I am always dressed in black, which makes it more difficult to notice stains and I have a scented key chain hanging from my rear-view mirror masking the smell of blood and death. I will admit it does a decent job.

The officer approaches, and I lower the window, smiling innocently when I say.

"Hello officer! May I ask why I am being stopped?"

He smiles back, which is a good sign.

"Hello, sir. License, and registration, please. The weather will get really bad. We are just informing people and checking if they have the necessary means to stay safe while driving."

He informs me and then quickly adds.

"Nothing to worry about; your car seems to be completely by code."

He checks the papers I have handed him again before he hands them back to me.

"Where are you going this late?"

He questions and I chuckle. *I am just disposing a body officer; nothing to be concerned about.*

"I am visiting my girlfriend, going to surprise her. I can open the back if you want to check the vehicle."

I bluff, hoping he won't really ask for that. *I only have a body back there, nothing to be suspicious about sir.*

He shakes his head, relief washes over me.

"No need, be safe and have fun!"

He tells me and he walks away.

"Have a good night!"

I call as he walks away and starts the car again. I sent another message: **milk is secured.**

I continue driving, checking from time to time to see if I am being followed. Luckily enough, the officer hasn't been following me since he stopped me.

As I reach the abandoned property we have chosen as a dumping site, I park and open the back, dropping the body bag over my shoulder. I take my shovel in my hand. I start hiking up the hill surrounded by woods and nothingness.

I checked the area for a week before we started hunting in this town. We have a set of rules, designed to keep us out of the eye of the law. No more than five women per town. Never dispose of the bodies in the same area we hunt. Always research both the hunting grounds and the dumping site, for a week before we start. Make sure it is remote. Always pay cash. Never, get close enough to the locals. Don't draw attention. Blend in.

For the most part, we have been really good at following the rules. We have never had issues, never even been suspected. Once, years ago, we had a body being discovered but was pinned to a serial killer who was active in that area. It was one of our first games; we were still learning, evolving, if you may.

I reach the top of the hill and pause for a moment to take in the view. The rain is now pouring harder, and I am getting wet. I am pretty sure that if the rain continues, it will hide most evidence of my being here.

I continue my path, going deep into the woods surrounding the property. A house is located where I have parked, but it has been empty for years. I have done my research. The owners died around twenty years ago, and there were no living relatives to take on the property.

It remained abandoned and forgotten, which makes it the perfect place since it is surrounded by wild nature and enough trees to shield me from the world while I dig.

I don't walk too far from the property, there is no need for that. I pick a spot under a tree, and I have three relatively fresh holes with bodies in them next to it. *You will have company in your afterlife sweetie.* I think, and I must be crazy talking in my head to a dead woman. If anything else wasn't enough of a clue of my insanity, this should be it.

I place her on the ground and put my headphones on, picking a song to keep me entertained. I start digging, while metal music is filling my ears and thoughts are circling my mind.

It takes me around an hour to dig a deep enough grave, and throw the body bag inside, before I start filling the hole with dirt again. When I am satisfied with how much is filled I smooth the ground, I take the edge of the shovel and poke little holes in the ground all over her resting place.

I dig in my pocket and find a little bag with flower seeds. I sprinkle them inside the holes I made. A little gift for her. A sign of remorse on my part. She will never be found, but at least she will have some pretty flowers to keep her company. Alongside three more women, that are buried here as her neighbors. I throw some more dirt on top covering the seeds.

I take the path to my car, carrying the shovel while blasting music through the headphones. The sky is almost bright enough like a day and thunders are making it even brighter.

I check my phone for the time, and I see I have just enough time for a little detour. Remember rule number six? Yeah, I have completely shattered that one this time. It wasn't my plan in any way, but when I met her, I couldn't keep myself from getting to know her.

For the most part, I haven't gotten that close. I have been keeping an eye from a distance. Sometimes I watch her work while I drink my coffee, some others checking her house or follow her home. I will admit, it is a little unorthodox. But it is the only way I can be close to her without putting myself and the guys at risk. I will take what little I can.

Right now, I need to see her. I put my shovel in the back and get in the driver's seat. I drive in the direction I arrived from a few hours ago. A part of me, the one that worries, checks cautiously for the police car that stopped me previously.

The other part, the twisted one, gets hard on the idea of danger almost. The image of her in my mind makes me excited while I drive to her house. She doesn't live far from where we have been staying, the boys won't know I stopped most likely.

I have been doing this for two weeks already, they haven't realized it so far. I also spend my mornings in the diner where she works, but that is something I do in every town. My own little ritual after a hunt.

I enjoy watching normal people going about their lives, and there is nothing more normal than the morning crowd of a diner in a small town. I usually stay in the realm of just people-watching but something this time has changed.

It might be because I feel lonely or she is just unique. It might be just the fact that I was bored or jealous of the guys having each other. I don't really look into what drove me to start stalking her. It doesn't really matter. The reason is lost in the madness of the situation.

It takes about three hours to drive back and ten minutes to reach her house once I reach the town's main road. It is already five in the morning, and I know her schedule well. If I am lucky enough, she will have her curtains open, giving me the perfect view from her backyard while she gets ready for her day.

I park two houses down the road and walk to hers, jumping over the fence into her yard. I walk right to the spot under her window and look up.

Jessica is already up, and her curtains are open, as I was hoping. She is brushing her hair in front of her mirror, wearing only a lace thong and a t-shirt that is cropped right before her belly button. Her body is toned with muscles from working all day on her feet, and I know for a fact she hasn't worked out a day in her life or ever watched her diet. She is curvy where it counts and has a light shade of tan, remaining from the summer sun.

Her long curly hair reaches her waist and she gathers it all in a ponytail, leaving out two framing pieces strategically placed around the front of her face. She has no ink on her, and I love how clean and innocent she looks.

She has the most beautiful, piercing blue eyes I have ever seen that hold a glimpse of sorrow behind them. I often wonder what happened to her. I had tried to keep myself from asking around, but quickly enough, the curiosity took over.

She is putting her uniform on, and now it is time for me to leave. I walk back to my car; I need to get back to the house before the guys realize I am taking too long. I open the driver's seat and get inside, checking my phone. No messages. They are pretty busy, I bet. Good, I don't need them asking questions.

Mike

I follow my boyfriend as he drives in front of me on his own motorcycle, along the familiar path that leads to our favorite take-out place. We just had one of our little games, and I am still pumped with adrenaline. I can't wait to get home.

My cousin is driving behind us; he honks once before he turns left onto the highway leading to the next town. He is on a task of his own while we get some time alone to recharge, among other things.

It takes us five minutes to get to the place. Everything is too close in this town; it gets annoying. I am already ready to leave, the hunts almost feeling uneventful.

I am starting to wonder if eventually they will stop satisfying me, and I will need to find another way to cope with the darkness that clings to my soul. *A problem for another day,* I remind myself, as I park my bike next to Nate's. He has already walked inside and is now is looking at the menu, even though we are always ordering the same thing.

In every town we have been to, in every burger place we have visited, he always gets a cheeseburger with extra pickles, fries, and a strawberry milkshake. He has been getting the same thing since he was seventeen, when we would sneak around on little dates, living in our small hometown.

Both in the closet back then, we would pretend to be friends while we were holding hands under the table and experiencing stolen kisses in dark alleys. We always picked food from a burger place we used to love and would sneak into his house before Liam and I even lived there.

I am pretty sure his parents always knew, or at least suspected, but they never said anything. Nate himself never actually came out to them, a choice I always respected. I never cared who knew; it is none of their business who I fuck or who fucks me.

We haven't ever talked about labels, and I am pretty sure we don't need to, but from time to time, we had women join us. We both are into them, but find more in each other.

He orders his burger, and I order the same, minus the milkshake. I ask for a soda instead, and he looks at me like it is weird. Even though I get the same every time. We are both creatures of habit, and even though it has been years since we started dating, we still give each other trouble for our taste in food.

A way to keep things interesting and fun between us. Nate always complains about my taste in movies, and I complain about his taste in music. I always make fun of him for his milkshakes, but I dip my fries in them, and he is pouting when I do. Small things that only the two of us share.

We pick up our food and walk back to our bikes. I take the bag with mine, and he takes his as we both ride back to the house we have been renting for the past two weeks.

Ten minutes later, I am following Nate inside our house. *Everything is so damn close in this town.* My cousin's dog lifts his head but completely ignores us, going back to sleep.

This dog is only reacting to Liam, and I chuckle before I say.

"Hello to you too, buddy, glad to know you care if we return or not."

The dog clearly ignores me, and Nate shakes his head in disapproval of my grudge against the poor animal.

"You are crazy, you know that, right?"

He says, laughing.

I wink at him before I reply.

"Of course, I know; this is why you love me, though."

He doesn't say anything else; we get to the living room, and he removes his jacket. He places it carefully on the couch. He sits in his usual seat, and I flop on the floor next to him. We open our food, spreading it on the living room table.

"It is four women with tonight's hunt."

Nate tells me, and I know the look on his face too well.

He is about to say it is time to move. We have been reaching the limit faster in each town lately.

I take a bite of my burger and mumble back at him.

"I am pretty sure nothing will happen if we go over the limit for once."

He is not happy about my statement.

"Yeah, maybe you are right."

He responds and takes a bite of his food.

I open my laptop and search for my favorite TV show. *He hates that show.* I click play and start pretending I am focusing on the episode. He doesn't say anything else, knowing this is my way of telling him that the conversation has ended.

His phone vibrates halfway through the episode, and I see him as he checks his messages.

"Liam has been stopped by a police officer."

He informs me. He doesn't respond to the message, sets his phone down, and we both remain silent for the whole ten minutes it takes before the next text from Liam arrives.

He opens the message and turns to me.

"All good; he ditched them."

A sense of relief immediately reaches me. I wouldn't care less if I got caught, but I would hate my cousin going down for it. He is the less evil of all three of us. I would do anything to protect him, and for a long time, I did.

Liam

I arrive at the house when the first ray of sunshine hits. I notice the motorcycles parked in the driveway; the guys are already home. As I enter through the door, my dog comes running to greet me.

"Hello buddy." I say, as I pet him, his tail is wiggling like crazy and he licks my hand to thank me for the treat I just offered him.

My clothes are soaked with blood and mud from digging the grave. I have always been the one to dispose the bodies. Except of the first one, that was all Nate. The guys love the thrill of killing the women, but I personally enjoy the chase more.

I always had an eye for detail, I think better in crisis mode. That alone makes me the perfect option for that tedious task. My cousin Mike is too unpredictable to be trusted with that. Nate, his boyfriend, and my best friend is in charge of our finances. Leaving me with the clean-up duties. I remove my shoes, and now Dog is settling in his bed by the door.

"Good boy." I praise him, giving him one last pat on his head, before walking into the living room.

"That took more time than usual." Mike comments when he sees me.

"Yes, I had some complications, nothing to worry about." I tell him while passing through the living room, walking to my room. I have already let them know about the police incident.

I have no desire to admit that I took a little detour, to check on Jessica. Her existence must remain hidden from them.

We have been moving from town to town since we graduated college. We don't stay long enough to make any friendships, and we usually avoid drawing much attention to ourselves.

Even though It is our third week in this town. We have been hunting for two of them. It won't be long before we need to move on, and I would like to keep her a secret for as long as I am able to. I usually don't interact with women or anyone in fact. *Rule number six.* My little routine, of people-watching while drinking my coffee, and enjoying a piece of pie at the local diner in every town we have visited so far, is my own moment of peace.

We all follow the rules religiously. For the longest time, this has worked so well that I have been worrying fate will catch up with us soon. Maybe we will make a mistake or get bored. Mike might eventually have a mental breakdown, and burn the whole town to the ground. Whatever it will be, I doubt we will remain undetected forever, which is exactly why I allowed myself to indulge in this obsession, I have developed with the waitress of the cozy diner, I spent my mornings in over the past two weeks.

This time everything is feeling a little bit off. We are already close to the limit for this town. Mike is getting more restless every day as the anniversary of his family's death is fast approaching. We were ten years old when his family got killed in a car accident, he was the only survivor. My father was not that happy to take him in but there was no other choice.

My entire family was killed five years later in a fire. The police deemed it as a tragic accident, and we were placed in the foster care system.

We had met Nate earlier that year, a boy two years older than us and our only friend in school. He convinced his family to foster us and his parents later adopted us, making the three of us the heirs of their millions.

They passed away around a decade ago. Even though they were around for just a handful of years, I always felt like they were the only family we truly had.

Both guys are now are sitting cuddled up on the couch watching something on the laptop, and I find the perfect time to clean myself up before I head to the diner for my morning coffee.

I step into my bathroom turning the shower on while I remove my clothes and toss them in a garbage bag to dispose of later. I never keep my clothes after a hunt, only my leather jacket.

As I enter the shower the hot water hits my skin; there is a moment of relief from all the guilt that gathers in my soul every night after a chase. Even though I enjoy our twisted game as much as the others, I still find myself feeling some regret afterward.

The water is now turning cold; I have been lost in my thoughts of what seems like forever. I exit the steaming bathroom and grab a towel to wrap around myself as I go through my clothes, picking up what to wear has always been my favorite part of the morning.

As I finish getting dressed, I get down the stairs to the living room passing through it on my way out. I notice the guys are still in the same spot.

"I am heading out."

I announce and Mike nods.

I see Nate, as he gets up, turning his back to me, he walks to his own room shedding his clothes along the way. And I know too well what that means, that's their favorite part of the morning.

Mike and Nate constantly danced along the boundaries of their friendship, always finding exactly what they needed to fulfill their desires in each other. The thrill of the chase is what fills all of us with excitement, the adrenaline, the game of life and death. The guys find that oddly erotic in their weird sadistic way.

A year after we finished college, we began this game. The first girl was a coincidence. Mike was flirting with her at a party, and she angered him. He tied her up, put her in the back of his car, then brought her to the property where we were living at the time.

It was Nate's idea to grab the bikes and chase her, but it was never intended for her to die, it was more like teaching her a lesson. That happened accidentally when she dared to taunt Mike while running for her life.

It was like a switch flipped and I had that boy who held a gun over my father's head in front of me all over again. Mike's eyes had a spark, I only saw in him when he was killing someone, almost like it gets him off but not quite. I figured later what truly got him off was blowing off some steam after the kill while the hype of the chase was still in his system. Like he read my mind he gets up, and follows Nate to his bedroom, those two will be busy for a while.

I give Dog one last treat, and I walk out of the door. Reaching in my back pocket, I fish out my keys, and I get on my motorcycle. The drive to the diner is not long, and the gloomy morning is the ideal scenery for it.

I always enjoyed the mornings after it rained all night. I will admit the rain made things complicated for me last night, but it also works to my advantage as it covers any mistakes I might have made along the way. I made sure to erase my tracks as I was leaving the scene.

It was still raining when I reached Jessica's house. She was just getting up, even though it was barely five in the morning. I watched her from her bedroom window as she got ready for the day before I headed home to clean up, giving her enough time to open the diner.

But now I can't wait to see her again. I have been searching for a way to talk to her more, get to know her, even though I know I shouldn't. We won't be here for long, and regardless of how much I would love to have more of her, I know I can't.

Mike

As I walk into the bedroom the sound of water greets me, he is in the shower and I don't lose a moment shedding my clothes, as I enter. I step into the shower with him and he turns to face me with a smirk.

"Hello pup." His voice sultry and full of meaning, my gaze falls to his cock which is already getting hard and I grab him from the back of his neck pulling him close, crashing my lips on his. I take a step back and his body presses me against the wall, his kiss deep while his hand works my cock, stroking me as it grows in his hand.

"Turn around."

He barks and I obey.

"Yes sir."

"Good boy."

He praises me and I hear the lube bottle's sound, *he was expecting me to join him*, as he squirts the liquid on his hand. I replace the hand he had on my cock with my own and lean on the shower wall, pressing my ass against his length. A finger enters me, prepping me with lube and I reach with my other hand to stroke him.

He bites my neck and praises me.

"Good pup."

I'm moaning and pushing against his hand impatiently.

"Fuck me."

I say, as if he didn't need anything more he enters me with a hard thrust and I press my ass impaling myself on his dick.

His thrusts are getting harder and faster and he growls in my ear.

"You feel so good puppy."

His hand is now stroking me holding mine firmly on my cock and I am about to come as I feel him getting close himself. He spills inside me and my release coats the shower wall. *This man is a fucking god.*

After our shower Nate decided to take a nap, my man needs his beauty sleep. While I, on the other hand, decided I needed to find our next victim.

I have always been the one to locate our victims, Liam is in charge of cleaning up afterwards and does the background check making sure their disappearance will go unnoticed until we leave town. Nate is the one who keeps our bank accounts full, running the family business while we travel. In addition to all these, Liam usually stalks them for a few days prior to kidnapping them. I personally think this is a bit unnecessary, but he is a control freak and gives him a sense of security.

My process usually is simple: I go through the websites of local businesses and check their feed for women that fit our type. I don't think the guys know the reason behind that specific type of woman we hunt, since I am pretty sure if it wasn't for me, they would not even do that anyway. I am sure my cousin suspects it though.

I find nothing in the usual pages, and I decide to look through the local church's events. Usually, those are not the best way to go about it, since women who hang around these events are older than our age range.

I open the post of a recent event and I pause. I am looking at one of the pictures, a bunch of people in it but one particular woman stands out. Her jade green eyes, so bright, practically glowing. Those eyes I am well familiar with. Those eyes that I used to feel would protect me from everything bad in the world, the same that caused me so much pain. *The woman is the spitting image of my mother.*

The laptop slips off my hands and lands on the floor making enough noise for Nate to come running.

"What happened?"

He questions, his eyes traveling between myself and the shattered screen.

I can't talk. I am not sure if I am even breathing. *I saw her die. That woman is not her. I saw her die.* I repeat to myself over and over again, like it will make everything okay again.

My mother was a cruel woman, she used to punish me, starve me, and hit me for the fact her husband liked the little boy in his house more than his own wife.

She looked the other way when he was coming to my room at night. It was only a couple of years before their accident. Enough to hunt me for a lifetime. He created demons, I have never quite found the way to satisfy, and even though he was the one responsible for that, I hated her as much for turning the other way and punishing me instead of protecting me.

Liam

Jessica is working, I have been here every day she worked this week. She has been my new secret addiction. I enter the busy diner ignoring everyone in my path as I head to the remote booth at the end of her section.

I take the seat next to the window, but I rarely look outside while being here. My focus is always on the brunette, serving customers and smiling politely to everyone, while she barks orders to the cook and the other servers.

She is a fucking hurricane, storming across the diner like she owns the place. I have asked around and gathered information about her even though this is risky enough for me to be here. Let alone asking about the young woman in her twenties.

I am not much older than her from what I have gathered. She is twenty-six years old and has been in this town her whole life, raised by a single father although I wouldn't call it exactly that. The guy hasn't kept a job since Jessica was sixteen and before that, he had a series of short-lived jobs after her mother's passing.

A truly tragic story this one, and I am not strange to those. Jessica has been raising herself more than likely since she was ten. She did a well damn job if you ask me. Even though she is now working at a meaningless job, she is as good as the owner here, running the place.

The sweet brunette with the stunning smile approaches my booth to take my order, and my breath stops. Her scent captivates my senses and for a moment, I forget why I am here, and the only thing I want to do is to bend her over that table and claim her as mine, letting everyone know who she belongs to. She doesn't belong to me, though, and I am well aware of that.

"Hello, what can I bring you today?"
she asks, her voice dripping sweetness.
"How about a cup of coffee and a piece of that cherry pie? The smell alone has been haunting me since I walked in."

I tell her, and she smiles, a smile I believe is a mask at this point that she puts on every time she enters through the front door.

She leaves to fetch my order and I take the time to check my phone. An unread message is flashing on the screen, and Nate's words come across the moment I open it.

Don't be late. Mike is getting restless and he has found the next one.

This is too soon, I just buried the one from last night a few hours ago. We never hunt two nights in a row.

I type a simple **okay** and send the message right in time for Jessica to appear with my order.

"Thank you sweetheart."

I take some money from my wallet and hand her the bills, always making sure to tip her more than enough, sometimes more than my order costs in total. She needs the money, and I have enough to spare. Nate's parents made sure we were more than set for our entire life and their son made sure to double the inheritance in the course of the first three years after their death.

It would be a lie to claim that having money isn't something that comes in handy when your main form of entertainment is hunting women for sport before you kill them. We have never been caught but even if we did I am sure, it will be nothing a well-paid lawyer couldn't fix.

Every now and then, we even take breaks and attend social events in New York maintaining our image as businessmen. In reality, though Nate is the only one doing everything when it comes to the family business, me and Mike are mostly the faces of it. Mike is twisted and psychotic, but he is also extremely charming. Women drop at his feet if only they knew, what he likes to do to his women.

We always had one rule though about the women. We never touch the ones we hunt, in a sexual way. None of us are into that type of evil. Of course, the guys are well satisfied with each other and I haven't found a need for a woman in years, until Jessica, that is.

As the thought crosses my mind, I see her exit through the back door next to the kitchen, a fact I know means she is on her break. I wouldn't usually do this but today I decide, I need more than three words from her and I quickly follow her making sure no one notices me as I slip through the staff-only section of the diner and out of the door.

The moment I walk through the door, I see Jessica leaning on the stone wall of the alley that leads to the backside of the restaurant. She smiles when she sees me.

A cigarette is settled between her lips, and she takes a deep drag off of it, releasing the smoke as her eyes wander to the busy road at the end of the alley.

"This is really bad for you." I say, breaking the silence between us.

"I am pretty sure, I am a grown-ass woman. I can make my own decisions."

she spats back and her spark makes my dick twitch in my pants.

I stalk closer to her, and I feel her body tense; her eyes rise to meet mine, and I can see her clench her thighs together. My presence is getting to her as much. I brush my lips against her neck, my breath making the hair on her skin rise. She holds her breath, the cigarette falling from her lips and I can feel her pulse rise as I push my body against hers.

"I tried to stay away from you." I mumble more to myself than her and I see a smirk form on her lips.

"I was hoping you wouldn't."

She tells me, and her hand curls on the fabric of my t-shirt pulling me closer to her. She crashes her lips against mine and I kick her legs open.

My hand falls between her legs and I find that wet spot on her soaking underwear .

"You are so wet for me sweetheart."

I notice, my voice dripping with lust and I feel her take a husky breath before she talks.

"I want you to fuck me."

Her request is a godsend and I can't wait to be inside her. I push the flimsy fabric of her underwear to the side, and one of my fingers enters her tight pussy. A sweet moan slips her lips, as a second and a third finger joins the first.

I feel her come undone against my hand, as she tries to ride it, basically fucking herself, with my fingers trying to reach her orgasm.

"Good girl." I praise her.

"Such a needy girl aren't you."

She nods and I think she has lost her ability to talk altogether. She moans and bites my shoulder trying to keep silent.

"Come for me sweetheart."

I say and it is not long before I feel her pussy spasm against my hand.

"Good girl." A much-needed praise slips my lips and she is trying to grasp her breath when I remove my hand from inside her.

"I want to be inside you." I inform her.

She nods.

"Yes please."

The only thing, she manages to say. The only thing I needed. I unbuckle my belt and unzip my pants. I fist my cock and pump it twice, before I line up with her entrance. I lift both her legs and she wraps them around my waist. I get inside her pushing both of us against the stone wall.

She moans and claws on my neck, sending shots of pain through my core, as I fuck her hard and fast. I can tell, she is close again and I can't thank my luck enough, my own orgasm is close approaching.

"Come for me sweetheart."

I order her and her body obeys, as she rides the wave of her orgasm moving her body, to take me deeper.

"Fuck please I can't."

She tries to complain as I keep fucking her sore pussy and she moans against my lips as I kiss her.

It is not long before my own orgasm comes, spilling inside her. She milks my cock taking every drop as she comes around it for one more time, and I can't keep myself from biting her lip, sending a little bit of pain through her. Her legs fall to the ground, my cock slips out. She straightens her underwear and her uniform back in place .

"That was incredible." She tells me and I smile. She lights another cigarette and offers it to me.

"Indeed it was." I agree with her, shaking my head at the cigarette. This was never my thing.

"I will see you around, Jess." I tell her as I walk back inside, leaving her in the alley.

Jessica

That was not how I planned my break, but this man has something; I don't know. His energy attracts me like a moth. The mysterious guy who started coming to my work two weeks ago and has been captivating my thoughts every waking moment of my existence since.

We never got that close before today; something felt different in many ways. When he joined me on my break, my expectations were as low as my standards, but he definitely did more than meet them.

I remember the first time he entered through the diner's front door. It was a rainy day and busy as hell. Lucy, the other waitress who usually works with me on Sunday mornings, had called off.

Her child was sick, and I understand more than anyone the importance of family. Mostly because I know how it is to lose one. But it was rather inconvenient to work a busy shift on my own.

My mood changed the moment he arrived. He showed up, with a gloomy look in his eyes and didn't really look around. That was until he raised his eyes to meet mine, when I approached him for his order. It feels like his eyes never left me from that moment. He always observes me in silence while he drinks his coffee.

He doesn't order much, but he is clearly not struggling for money. I am pretty sure his order is based on preference. He drinks his coffee black and always orders a piece of pie.

Some days it's cherry; others it's lemon, but he always takes exactly five bites before he sets the plate on the side and spends the rest of the time watching me work. He is always early, but not too early and spends at least half his day here.

He never asks for a refill on his coffee, and I am pretty sure it is to be polite. He will always accept one if I offer. He tips more than he should, and his smile can make my knees buckle. It can stop time and make everything silent.

Everyone becomes noise when he is around. It would be an understatement if I said I wasn't hoping for what happened today, for weeks since the first time I saw him. That he will never know.

He is dressed in expensive clothes, but his look is almost unkempt. A worn leather jacket, with a pair of jeans and some type of t-shirt, is his usual attire. Almost, like it is some type of uniform he picked for himself.

His hair is curly and slightly longer on the top, but shaved on the sides. His pale skin is decorated with beautiful colors of ink, flowers, and co-webs decorate his neck and hands. He has deep green eyes, a contrast to his pale skin and dark hair. They look like a shade between forest and jade green, almost like a mix of dark and light shades. I haven't seen such unique eyes before.

He is always polite, and if you told me that man would be so passionate, as I experienced a few moments earlier against that wall. I would laugh.

I see him sitting in his regular seat now, while I continue to work. Still feeling his cum leaking out of me. A little secret between the two of us, that none of these people suspect.

The day passes quickly and when my shift ends, as I am about to leave my eyes drift to the booth in the corner of the diner, in hopes of seeing him for one last time before I head out. He is not there.

As I step outside, though my curiosity about his location is satisfied, seeing him leaning against his bike, I make sure to ignore him, not wanting to give him more than I should. I get in my car, and not even one look is shared between us. I drive to my house, a short distance that I would usually walk instead, but this morning I chose to take the car, being too tired to deal with walking.

A few moments later, I am parking in our driveway and mentally preparing myself to enter my house. My father should be passed out by now. He is mostly spends his days drinking, and by the time I am back from work, he is either too drunk to notice or in a deep sleep in his armchair. Sometimes I find him on the floor between his bedroom and the bathroom, others he is peacefully napping on the top step of the stairs.

Today it seems like I am lucky. I notice as I get to the top floor of the old house, that he must be in his room. I don't see him in his usual spots. *Good, today was hard enough already.*

I thank my luck silently and move to my bedroom, going straight away for the connected bathroom. I turn the water on, pouring some bath soap and salts in the fast-filling tub. *A hot bath is the best way to finish this day.*

Liam

I wait, leaning on my bike for her shift to end. I see her leave the diner, and walk to her car. She knows I am still here, but does nothing to show it. *Smart girl.*

Her taste still lingers on my tongue, and her scent is as vivid in my mind. I want more of her but today is not the day for that. I am already late. I check my phone, luckily I have no messages or calls from Nate yet.

I wait for a minute or two, giving her a head start while she drives toward her house, and I follow from a distance not visible to her.

I have been doing the same thing every afternoon, whether we hunted the night before or not.

Something about this woman captivates my interest and even though she would be the ideal prey for our little game, I am selfish enough to not share her with the others yet. *After all, her death would bring me no joy.*

My phone buzzes and I answer the call while driving, Nate's voice coming through the ear bud.

" When are you coming home? Mike is being restless."

He tells me and I chuckle.

"What, fucking his ass all morning, did not help with his attitude?"

Nate's irritation is clear through the phone. He takes a moment before he answers.

"Just come home, so we can plan this."

The call drops, and Jessica just pulled into her driveway. I don't stop. I continue down the road, switching to the route for the house we have been staying in for the past month.

The owners of that house were too happy to rent it, after years of being unoccupied, and did not do much screening of their new tenants. We always pick places like that, make sure to pay cash, and avoid giving any real information about ourselves.

Nate's family provided more than enough to sustain us for years after their passing, without the need to work. But what truly supports our lifestyle is their son's investing skills. For the record, we had nothing to do with that. They were already old when they had him and died happily in their beds a few months apart from each other. We loved them as much as they loved us.

I would truly say that the old couple was the only family Mike and I truly had. They took us in when no one else would, got us through college, and made sure we were set for life and all that, only because their son fell in love with the hungry, skinny boy my cousin once was.

It is already getting dark when I arrive at the house, having spent most of the day at the diner. Nate is talking on the phone with someone in a language I don't recognize, and I am pretty sure it is business-related. He is the one in charge of our income for a reason.

Mike is pacing up and down the hallway, and Dog -yes, I named my dog Dog - circles around him with a wagging tail. Mike looks stressed and I can tell he is getting restless. *Nate was right about that.*

His shoulders look tense, and his hair is wet; I am not sure if he just got out of the shower or if Nate attacked him by throwing water at him to calm him down. But I would not put it past the two of them for either to be true.

"Mike, are you doing okay, buddy?"

I ask without really expecting an answer. Mike stops and looks at me, his head tilts to the side, and a moment passes before he answers.

"Yeah, yeah, fine."

I am not sure if he even heard my question. I know how he gets some days.

My cousin, although I adore him, has his demons, and it is not unusual that they take hold of him, and everything he sees is red.

"Nate?"

I call his boyfriend's name in hopes of some explanation of why my cousin is so disoriented, but Nate ignores me, waving his hand at me in a dismissive way. *You are being so helpful right now, dude; thank you.*

"I found the next prey."

Mike tells me.

He is showing me a woman's picture on his phone, and I see why he is being so weird. The woman is a spitting image of his mother, and even though we once believed my aunt was the perfect angel of a mother, after Mike got rid of my father and the rest of my family met their end in that fire, he told me how wrong everyone was about his mother. She abused him in more ways than one, letting her husband have a piece of him, looking the other way. His mind was locked in a dark place for years before he found a way to cope. *Killing. That is how he manages.*

Nate once told me that Mike in one of his deranged moments confined him, with the truth about his parent's accident. Mike one night was so fed up with his mother's ignorance and his stepfather's behavior that decided to cut the brakes of their car causing the accident that took them out.

A boy, of the age of ten, searched the internet for how to cut the brakes of the car, and staged the accident. That is how much impact their abuse had on him. He was also in the car with his sister, who tried to shelter by putting his body over hers, when the car flew off the bridge. He tried to cut her seat belt to help her escape the car, but the water was filling fast, and her seat belt was stuck. He tried and tried, but then it was a choice of his life or hers, and a young Mike decided to put his life over hers. *One could say, that was the time the Mike we know now was born. That decision forever haunts him.*

I have been sitting for hours in the living room trying to talk Mike out of hunting this woman and coming up empty. His mind is set. He is like a bull only seeing red from the moment her picture came up on his screen.

"Okay we at least need to do this right."

Nate tells him and Mike eventually nods, *good we are finally getting through to him.*

"We are going to do the process like with any other woman."

I add and he nods again.

"Tell me everything, you have gathered so far."

I say, hoping I can find something in what he will provide to convince him against this. He gives me a paper with an address and a name.

"Mary Smith."

I read her name out loud, and I see his leg bounce nervously.

"When are you going to start stalking her?"

He asks me, avoiding eye contact.

"First thing tomorrow, I need to do some research first. You know the process."

I tell him, and he seems satisfied enough, as he gets up to leave.

He turns for a moment to face me .

"Okay, I am going to sleep." He announces only looking at me and walks to his room.

I wait long enough for the door's clicking sound, indicating it is shut behind him, and turn to Nate.

"Do you think it is a good idea?"

He shakes his head.

"No, I believe it is a terrible idea."

He takes a sharp breath, his voice now low, barely coming out. "He is going to spiral, either way. May as well satisfy his request."

He explains.

I am fully aware he is right. Mike is not going to change his mind. He won't let it go. This woman will die either way. It will be in our best interest, if we do this right. I open my laptop and search for her name and address. I find a couple of social media accounts under her name. I search through the list to find the correct one.

I see with the corner of my eye that Nate is now walking to his own room. *Not Mike's.* He is giving him space, taking the opportunity to get some sleep of his own in the process. Good,

I need to have my focus on this task if we are going to do it without getting caught.

Mike will be more unpredictable than usual. The woman's appearance is clearly a trigger for him. The more we plan this, the better the chances that he won't get the police involved in our business.

I get my notebook and start writing down the info I gather about her. I find several people tagged in her photos, and someone that I assume is an ex-partner from the way he hugs her waist in every picture.

I check the dates and the pictures with that man. They are all dated four years ago. I switch tabs and check for the Man's profile. He is married to a woman and lives in Ohio. According to his profile status, he has been married for two years. It is entirely possible he is a past relationship of this woman.

I run a program between the two profiles to identify any interactions, and the last public messages appear to be five months before his wedding. It is safe to assume he won't be an issue. He is clearly out of the picture for good.

Next, I check her workplace listed on her social media. She is working from home, listed as a remote worker in their list of employees. That means it will take at least a week before someone suspects her missing from her work environment.

Next step after checking her work, is to go back to the closest friends list. I have already written down a list of names from her pictures, and now I am going through them one by one. I am running the same program I used for the married guy; the ones whose communication has been at least a year ago, are getting crossed out. I make a second list of names; those are the ones she has been communicating with recently.

I go to their pages and mark in my notes those who live in different areas; that will probably mean, they have only online communication with her. I am able to get the list down to the three people she is contacting regularly and might notice her missing. As I finish with the list of friends, colleagues, and possible partners, my focus turns to her activities in her everyday life. I need to learn every detail of her routine before I start stalking her.

This is easy, she is mostly staying home. Works from home, has a cat, and doesn't like to drink or party. Given the fact she is a little older than our usual target preference when it comes to age, that part seems to be to our benefit.

The older a woman is, the more people she might have in her life and might miss her. Younger people tend to be more carefree, hence why they might live a more complicated lifestyle, and communicate with their close friends and family more sporadically.

She is spending her nights reading and has multiple Instagram posts with a mug of tea next to a book, all with a timestamp around six to nine in the evening. I check her work hours again, and it makes sense. She is done with work by four.

It is safe to say she is living a lonely life; not many people will miss her. It will take more than a week for anyone to report her missing, and since we are already in our limit for this town with her included. We will be long gone before anyone does.

Mike

This morning can not be more complicated than it is right now. It is not even morning anymore. My mind is stuck between the past and the present, and I feel lost in more ways than one. I used to think my mother was my safe haven, and until I reached the age of eight, she truly was.

Then things changed, and the person I once believed would protect me from my nightmares looked the other way as the man she let into our lives created them.

I am looking at the laptop's shattered screen, which somehow still works. I am starting to think I must be delusional because the woman smiling with her family in those photos is the same exact woman I saw struggling to breathe, struggling to escape while the car was filling with water, sinking to the bottom of the lake. My sister, Lena, was never meant to be with us that night. They came to pick me up from football practice, and I made sure not to wear my seat belt and to let the window open on my side of the car.

My father had an idea to take us all out for dinner because my mother hadn't cooked again. She was in a spiral of her own, filled with drugs and alcohol, a way to ignore what was happening in her house every night. I learned to expect it; I tried locking my door, and I tried saying no. But I would never be able to keep him out of the room.

My plan was clear. *Perfect even.* I called my father, claiming Liam's dad would not be able to drive us home. Then I made sure to find an excuse for Liam to join another teammate's family on the way home instead.

While my mother and father were talking to my coach about the fight I started earlier, *a part of the plan as well*, I messed with the brakes of the car. No one would have known, but then I saw my sister running towards the car right before we were getting ready to leave. She had stayed behind for an art class that took place after school hours. My mother let her know that they would pick me up, so she could join us for a family pizza night.

I never intended for my sister's death, and it haunts me to this day, if I were to be honest, I would admit that this is probably why the game started: my need to numb my pain. The hunt is what does that for me, the sight of blood. Their screams, make her screams faint inside my head, and everything silences for a moment or two. And I need those moments as a man needs air.

Nate has always done everything in his power to make sure I survived every moment since we met. He started convincing his family to take us in, way before there was a need for it.

I knew about Liam's father's habits long before I went to live with them, and while I was planning to take out my useless mother and the monster I called my father, I already had a plan to end my cousin's nightmare as well. One would think, a kid can't be thinking that way, but I stopped being one, the first night after I turned eight. When he entered into my room and created the nightmare I was trapped in until his death.

My mind drifts back to the day the social worker brought me to their house. After spending two days in custody of the state while they were working on the specifics leading to assign me, my mother's brother as my legal guardian. His wife welcomed me with a smile but he was clearly not happy, he got another mouth to feed.

I had noticed the bruises Liam had, and how dark his eyes got when his father was around. His gaze full of terror told me everything he would never tell me. But it was that day my suspicion took root.

We were eating dinner and I had been starving for the two days before, because of the group home they had assigned me until they figured out who would get me. There were too many kids and not enough food for everyone. A small boy around the age of seven that looked incredibly skinny was sharing my room, and I made sure to give him every ounce of food I got.

He needed it more than I did. Not that I could eat, my sister's screams still echoed in my mind days after I witnessed her drowning. Her death is on my hands, and even though my parent's is too, she is the only one I regret.

The moment I finished my plate, what little my aunt had to spare. I asked in a low voice if I could have anything else. I was still starving. She got up to get me more, when her husband decided to get up and bang the table with both hands.

"You will be grateful for what we give you boy."

He said, his voice firm and rigged of authority. I remember the night like it was yesterday.

He approached me quickly on the other side of the table and pulled me off my seat by my shirt, ripping it in the process. *I loved that shirt Lena got it for me on my last birthday.*

His breath reeked of alcohol and he pushed me to the floor stepping on my back, he removed his belt and it wasn't long before I felt the worn leather, soaked with my cousin's blood, hit my own flesh.

I screamed. A scream full of rage. Tears filled my eyes with every lash, with every spiteful word that left his mouth.

"Your whore of a mother had to go get herself killed."

He said and I laughed inside my head. *Only if he knew.*

"Always having to bear the burden of her mistakes, stupid slut now had to dumb another useless boy on my lap."

He said, his voice echoed in the room, with nothing else but my screams and cries to fill the void in between.

"You are worse than the other one."

He said and I did not fully understand if he meant his own son but the words puzzled me for a while that night.

Liam

I have been thinking the first night Mike arrived to live with my family. It was past midnight when everyone had fallen asleep, and I entered Mike's room with a plate of food I had stolen from the kitchen and a first aid kit I kept hidden under my bed.

He had dared to ask for more food at the dinner table, and my father had let his anger on him. Even though I was used to that, seeing my cousin on the ground bleeding and screaming as my father's belt landed repeatedly on his bare back, broke something inside me. I always felt a strong bond with him. I was too weak to protect him that night, and every night that followed until the fire.

"Are you okay?" I asked him not really expecting an answer when I noticed his eyes glowing from all the tears but his face was not sad and he did not seem like he was in pain.

"We should kill him."

He said and at first, I thought he surely must be joking. But then the idea started to take root and I dropped next to him on the floor.

"Should we?"

I asked while helping him out of his t-shirt, noticing the blood stains on it.

"I have a plan." He told me, as I soaked a cotton ball with alcohol before I started cleaning his wounds.

"Those will need stitches." I told him, and he nodded.

"What is the plan?"

I inquired.

"We will need to find a way to keep everyone else safe and get a gun."

He said and continued.

"There is one in the safe of my house, that now belongs to me. It won't be hard to get access to it."

I took out the stitching kit I had asked a nurse to give me, after months of hospital visits with the same marks as the ones I was seeing on Mike's back in that moment.

The woman was so kind as to teach me how to stitch myself even though she was breaking a number of rules. I think deep down she knew if a boy around ten needed that knowledge, things were that bad, that it was a life and death situation.

My parents would not always take me to the hospital, sometimes took days of open wounds bleeding through my clothes before my mother would take me.

"This will sting."

I told him and I poked the needle through his skin, stitching it like a ripped hole in one of my t-shirts.

I saw his face twitching with every stitch and I worked my way trying to be quick. He said nothing more, but his face told me everything, each time the needle went through his skin. I finished, doing the best I could to make sure to keep the wound clean before I dressed it with a bandage.

Not another word was said between us that night. I gathered the rest of the first aid kit while he ate his food. We sat in silence both lost in thoughts until we fell asleep on opposite sides of the floor.

It was five years after when his plan was executed. Some mistakes happened along the way. We thought we had enough time to take everyone out but we barely made it ourselves, when the fire claimed the house. My father was lying on the floor, dead after Mike had shot him.

The man that is now in front of me reminds me so much of that boy, the same dark gaze full of rage. A cold expression is firmly placed on his face, while we are trying to change his mind again. His eyes though, those are on fire.

This is too risky, the woman looks too much like his mother. Even if he can handle it, in the case her body is found, it is entirely possible we will be brought up for questioning. Even though no one here knows our real names, for the most part at least.

That doesn't mean they can't link somehow the resemblance of his mother, and himself to the woman who showed up dead. Especially if a true crime freak gets interested in the local murder, in a town that hardly has anything happen that is remotely bad. This place is peaceful, the criminal activity is so low,I am surprised that we have been unnoticed so far.

It is not that hard to do a reverse image search, and the news from our town will come up with the face of Mike's mother front page, the day of the accident.

"Are you sure you want to choose that one?"

Nate asks once again, and we both know the question is rhetorical at this point. If Mike puts his mind on a victim that woman will die no matter what.

"Yes I want to do it tonight."

Mike answers him and I am quick to say.

"We never hunt so close to the previous one for a reason."

Reminding him of the rule we all agreed upon, the night after our first chase.

"Let me stalk her for a few days. I have been doing my research, while you and the pretty boy over there, got your beauty sleep."

I tell him before he can say anything else.

"I agree if we do it, we have to do it right."

Nate adds and Mike releases a defeated sigh.

"Fine, you can plan this but I want her dead."

He tells us and storms off once again.

The last forty-eight hours have been a roller coaster of constant fighting, and memory trips in nightmares, we both have tried to forget.

He seems to ignore both me and Nate, as he paces in the living room now. He is mumbling about something we both don't seem to be able to understand. My eyes meet Nate's and we both agree in silence, that we can not avoid this.

We started doing this for Mike. The hunt, the blood spill, and the rush, all seemed to calm him down in a way he needed more than anything.

We both love him more than anything to keep doing this until we either get caught or our own end arrives.

If we are going to do this we should do it right. I choose to go to my room for a few hours in hopes of sleeping until night-time.

I will start with her house. It will be easy enough to watch her, while she is going about her nightly activities. If I am lucky enough she will leave a window open; the weather is still hot enough during the afternoon time that she might need the airflow while she reads.

If everything goes according to plan, I will only need to observe her for a few hours and be able to squeeze in a little night trip to check on Jessica.

At least I know my girl always leaves her window open. I am wondering if she would continue doing that with the knowledge that I watch her sometimes while she is getting ready.

Something tells me she might be into it. Turns out she is quite a freak herself, letting me fuck her during her break the other day was something, I didn't expect. I know I am playing with fire, but I can't wait to see how much of a freak she can be.

Maybe hunting this woman is not that bad of an idea, if it gives me more time with Jessica. Just stall for a week, while gathering information on her. Nate might be successful in changing Mike's mind for once.

Liam

It is around nine when I finally arrive at the woman's house. Her name is Mary, and as I was expecting, she is sitting in her living room.

She has a bottle of wine open and a full glass next to her. *I was wrong about the drinking.* She is reading a book with her curtains wide open, and the only light in the room is the lamp over her head.

I chose a dark spot on her porch, and I have been sitting here for the last thirty minutes watching her.

I made sure you can't see me from inside or if you are passing from the street. I am good at hiding in the shadows. Right now, I would bet good money that I will spend a good amount of my time in this spot, the next few days.

She doesn't seem the type that leaves the house almost ever. I knew, of course, that much from her social media and my research so far, but sometimes the online image someone puts up is completely different from reality.

Some people like to portray a persona that isn't even the slightest bit close to reality on their social media. Either to get followers or to maintain whatever image they prefer in the online world.

Mary doesn't seem to have the need for it, and I thank my luck for this. I have no intention of putting in more effort than I need in this situation. I am already not comfortable with stalking a woman that reminds me of my aunt.

I can't say I have bad memories of my aunt. Amelia was always polite to me, and always made sure to make some extra food, when I would be over at their house. She would smile and play with us or take us for walks and playdates. It pains me that I got the nice side of her when my cousin suffered so much at her hands.

My memories of the woman who looks identical to the one I am now watching as she reads are full of summers and flowery scents. Smiles and happiness that didn't even resemble the darkness this woman had in her in the slightest.

Mike on the other hand, got her bad side. The one that starved him, beat him, and locked him in a closet, with no food or water or bathroom access for hours. The one that would let him go to school dirty, without lunch money. The one that would look the other way, when her husband would abuse him in every way he wanted.

She had Mike when she was a teen, and got married three years later. Mike never knew his dad, he died when they were engaged, before he was born. I think in a way Amelia despised Mike for that.

At least I can't think of any other reason a mother would let those things happen to her child. Her own flesh and blood. I would have never let anyone touch my own, if I had any, and I am a psychotic asshole that hunts people for sport. I guess even criminals have some morals, but this woman had none.

The night continues in silence as I watch Mary read her book. It is in the middle of the night when she finally decides to go to bed, and I am relieved of my duty.

I should really go straight home but instead, I find myself driving to Jessica's house. A desperate need to see her grows inside me. It is not a long drive before I am parking in my usual spot, behind a large tree in her backyard. I am not too worried about the lights being on in her living room.

More than likely, her father has passed out somewhere in there. He is too drunk to care for his life or his daughter. He would never notice any type of movement in his yard, even if my motorcycle was visible from his side of the house. I bet it isn't.

I know for a fact it is not from Jessica's room. I will admit I have sneaked in twice already, and checked for visibility. Her room even smells like her. It is decorated like a child's room, which makes it a little disturbing, that a grown woman still sleeps there.

From what I know about her, It is safe to assume her mother probably decorated it. Jessica seems to be the type, that holds on to memories for dear life. It makes sense why she hasn't changed the room during her teen or adult years.

I see now it is dark, and even though nothing is visible from where I stand I can almost see Jessica's sleeping form in her bed. Her bedroom is surrounded by a pink wallpaper with little teal flowers on it and porcelain dolls on the shelves.

When I was there, I noticed that those dolls must not have been moved since at least her mother's death. They are collecting dust, but the room itself is neatly cleaned and cared for. The comforter on her bed has the scent of some type of flower that I recognized well from its owner.

Scented candles are placed on her vanity and nightstand, the only things she has added since her childhood. The bathroom connecting to her room is also decorated with the same pink shades and flowers; bath salts and other skin care products are piled on the side of the bathtub. Fluffy pink and teal towels hang on her bathroom wall. They are matching the equally fluffy carpet that goes edge to edge in the entire bedroom and bathroom.

It is clear to me that this bedroom was designed with love; it doesn't match the rest of the house, which is unkempt and almost falling apart. It is as if Jessica has tried her best to keep the room as her mother had it. Keeping her memory alive in a way.

I am disappointed she is sleeping right now, I really needed to see her. I was expecting it though, when I drove here. She works for the better part of the day, and when she arrives home, she has to take care of her father.

It is reasonable that she would be sleeping early, considering the five a.m. start to her day.

Still, I can't keep myself from frowning at the idea that I am going to have to wait until morning to see her.

I am contemplating climbing that window and taking a peek inside, just to see her for a minute or two. Maybe tuck her into bed and kiss her goodnight. If she is tired enough, she might not notice me, but it is a stretch to believe that, and a risk I am not willing to take.

I am not sure why this woman's presence seems to be so addictive. I am not the type to lust after a woman. I have been alone for years with no interest in anyone. There was the occasional hookup in bars when we attended college or when we would visit New York, our home base. I always made sure not to get involved with anyone in the towns we hunted. Too much risk for no apparent reason, in my opinion.

I decide to drive home since Jessica is deep in her sleep, and the opportunity to see her has been missed. I get on my bike, glancing one last time at her bedroom window before I head back.

Mike,
the night of the fire.

"Wake up!"

I shake Liam's body, trying to wake him up from his sleep.

"What?"

He asks in his sleep and then his eyes fall on the gun in my hand. He quickly gets what I am about to do, and gets up from his bed.

We walk fast, with steady steps to the living room. His father has Liam's sister on the ground, his belt is in his hand and the poor girl is crying. He is usually hitting only Liam and me, but lately, his violence has been spread to his daughters. It is time, he needs to be stopped.

The girl sees me, as I approach him from behind. I am pointing the gun at him before I even talk. Her eyes grow wide. She is looking at me ready for what will follow.

"Get away from her!"

I order my voice steady and reeks of dominance. I am not sure where I have found this strength but it feels right. He has been tormenting us for years since I moved here, and I didn't wipe my entire family off existence, to trade one horror for another.

He turns to look at me, and chuckles at the sight of me and Liam with a gun.

"What do you think you are doing boy?"

He asks and I have nothing to say to him but I force myself to talk.

"Get on your knees or I will shoot!"

I tell him and he laughs in my face. I am not sure what comes to me since, I wasn't fully planning to shoot him. The plan was to scare him at first.

I don't wish to have more blood on my hands but I somehow find myself, pushing the trigger. The gunshot echoes through the house and I see his body fall on the ground. He gasps for air and I notice I got him where I am guessing his lungs are located.

I can't back out now. I turn to see Liam, his sister is now by his side and he clings to her hugging her tight as he nods to me. He forgives me for what I am about to do in silence, that's all I need.

I press the trigger again, and again. Until every bullet is now inside the man who has been slicing my flesh with his belt, every day for the past five years.

He's now laying there dead. I turn to my cousins.

"We need to burn the house. Make it look like an accident."

I declare and move quickly towards the kitchen. I open the cabinets, searching for the gasoline and alcohol, I know my aunt keeps for cleaning purposes.

"I will get the rest of them out!"

Liam calls, as I start pouring the liquid around the living room. His sister leaves in the opposite direction running towards the basement.

We both know what that means, her father has the little one locked in there again.

The flames start growing fast, and I am not sure why, but it feels like we are running out of time. I try to get to the basement to tell them to hurry but the staircase is now wrapped in flames. *Fuck, this is not how it was supposed to happen.*

"Liam, there is no time to save them."

He is standing next to me.

"They are coming down. Mom told me they will be right down!"

He claims but the flames are now approaching the stairs leading to the bedrooms, and I know for a fact we need to go now.

"Come on, we need to leave!"

I tell him, and I pull him through the flames trying to get to the exit. Liam is barely moving, his body is now stiff against my hold, as I am trying to get us both out. The door is burning with the rest of the house, and I am trying to think. *There must be another way out.*

I see my cousin, completely frozen in place, his eyes wandering in the flame-filled room. I am trying to think a way out, and my eyes fall on a chair that is not burning, next to a window. The flames haven't reached that part of the house yet but it won't be long before they do. I grab the chair and throw it out the window, breaking it in the process.

"Let's go."

I say and push Liam to climb out of the window.

He gets out and I follow behind. I am pulling his body along with mine, trying to reach the road. He is tripping and falling, I keep picking him up. *Just a few more steps buddy, we got this.*

He is crying and sobbing, falling to the ground the moment we reach the road. I know how he feels. My sister's death still haunts me like it was yesterday; his will too.

"We need to call Nate."

I tell him, and I hear sirens.

Quickly, the road is full of police cars and firetrucks and they are putting us in handcuffs. They are questioning us, Liam is not talking, and I am answering to the best of my ability.

I have thought about this moment countless times, and I have rehearsed what to say. I am making sure this looks like an accident. While Liam is standing here frozen, he is not crying anymore.

I managed to send a message to Nate right before they arrived, hoping he will find a way to take care of this. We have talked about this for months, I know he has been convincing his parents to take us in.

The plan was to make sure, Liam's mother flees with his sisters in case we couldn't stop his father without killing him. Liam had decided he would stay behind, and I had talked to Nate about it. He had offered us the opportunity to stay with his family, that is, what must happen now.

Burning the house to the ground with the entire family inside it wasn't part of the plan. I will forever regret it I am sure.

At least some sense of relief warms my heart, knowing that no man will hurt me or my cousin ever again.

I know he doesn't believe this right now. He won't believe it for years to come. In my twisted ways though, I only did this to save him. That, I will never regret.

Liam

It has been a week since I started stalking Mary. Mike's mind didn't change, and now I find myself in the back of the white colored van, while we drive the familiar path to her house. Nate is in the driver's seat as always with Mike on his side.

We park right outside, My cousin and I move quickly, as we exit the vehicle and run through her yard. We reach the door and the plan is simple. Mike is picking the lock, a skill he picked up years ago and I have my gun in my hand.

We wear masks, and we only remove them when we hunt them. None of them get out alive anyway, there is no reason to keep them on. But for this part, it is safest to do this. In case we missed someone living with them or someone sees us during the kidnapping.

Mary is sleeping in the same spot where she reads every night; a glass of wine is tipped over on the floor and the red liquid is spilled all over the floor. Her book is on her lap and now watching her up close, I can see how much she looks like my aunt.

I notice Mike's expression, as he seems frozen in place, his eyes are stuck on her face as well, and he is holding his breath.

"Come on, snap out of it!"

I tell him and he shakes his head trying to get some sense back in himself.

We need to do this now and fast, before one of her neighbors decides to call the police. So I walk towards the woman putting my gun in my waistband. I grab my knife, placing it on her throat.

"You will come with us."

I tell her and she nods to the best of her ability.

She is slowly waking up. Mike steps closer and picks up her body, she doesn't react or try to yell. We are usually expect some fight, but she looks defeated.

We walk out of the house, and I close her door to not raise suspicion, if someone sees the house from the road. Mike drops her body in the van and ties her up. He hops in the back with her and I take his place in the passenger seat.

"We are ready!"

He calls from the back banging the side of the van. A signal that we are ready to move. The car starts and we are heading to the maze. I look at Nate's face; he has a look that tells me he doesn't agree with tonight's hunt. *It will happen anyway.*

When we arrive at the maze, everyone gets out of the car. I hear Nate reciting the rules, and in a sense, it is like every other night, *but it isn't.*

The woman screams. She flees, and I see her black hair as the air brushes through it; she looks almost identical to my aunt, to the point that someone could think they were twins.

She is wearing a white summer dress, and the weather is getting cold. I am thinking it must be making things harder for her, but when adrenaline hits, all senses get dulled. I know that too well.

I noticed the green in her eyes, reminding me of my cousin's, almost comforting through the terror that the night has stored for her.

Even though I hate the kills, I love the chase just as much. The air brings chills to my skin and their screams make my dick hard. I know it is fucked up but, I can't keep myself from thinking my sweet Jessica in her place.

It takes a moment before I realize, I have her cornered and I get off my bike approaching her with a knife in my hand. I am ready to speak but she does instead.

"Liam?"

She asks, her voice low and I can tell she is shivering.
"What?" I ask, puzzled by the fact she knows my name.
She takes a moment before she asks.
"Are you Liam or Mike?"
I realize this woman knows both of us. Possibly from our childhood, back then the only way to tell us apart was Mike's blonde hair.

"I am Liam" I tell her and add "Who are you?"

She approaches me and her hand brushes my cheek.

"I am Mary, your mother."

She tells me and I think I must have heard wrong, but the look on her face solidifies her statement.

"Guys the hunt is over." I yell.

I help her on my bike; she doesn't speak a word while we drive back to the starting point. I see the guys approaching.

"What are you doing?"

Mike asks, but I ignore him, turning to Nate.

"Come with me."

I tell Nate and walk a little further, out of Mike's reach.

"Watch her."

I bark the order to my cousin.

I am not usually the one to show authority over our little group; that has always been Nate's role, but in desperate times... He follows, and I see Mike from the corner of my eye pacing around the woman. Something comes out of his lips but I am too focused on what I need to explain to Nate. The information I just got can't be perceived lightly.

Her statement was what I needed to piece everything together. How we always looked alike, how our birthday was the same day, there were no photos of my mother or aunt being pregnant from that year.

My father's words the first night Mike came to live with us, *Always having to bear the burden of her mistakes, stupid slut now had to dumb another useless boy on my lap.* I explain what Mary told me, and Nate nods in agreement with what we both think. We can't kill her, *yet.*

"Get her in the van pup!"

He orders Mike and me to see him obey, like a good boy as he always has.

Nate is the only person who can control this man. We get in the van and drive home; we need to figure this out before it gets too complicated. Before we get caught.

Nate

It has been almost two hours since we returned to the house. Mike is standing at the top of the basement's staircase, watching the poor woman we have in there. Her hands are still tied together, but she seems to have been in terms with the situation. She didn't try to leave when we arrived here, following willingly Liam to the basement. She hasn't tried to get free, she is just sitting there. Waiting.

I am standing next to Liam, on the other end of the hallway, leading to the basement's door. I am observing my man, as he is clearly losing his mind. So far he doesn't know what is happening or why we stopped the hunt. Liam and I hadn't had the courage to tell him.

"We need to tell him." Liam tells me, and I nod.

I know we need to; the problem is that I have no clue how or even what to tell him.

How do you tell a guy who killed his entire family, that it wasn't his family to begin with?

I wonder.

My phone's vibration snaps me out of that thought, and I see the email I just received. The background check for Mary. Liam did an excellent job, when we thought she was just another victim of ours, but we needed a professional to look into her.

Her story is a sad one and I am not sure if that makes it any better, but at least it makes my heart feel for her a little. I can only hope the chaos twins will have a similar reaction, maybe spare a life just once.

Liam, of course, has never been someone I have to worry about ending a life. The guy hasn't even killed once during the hunts. His *brother*, on the other hand, is definitely the one I need to worry about.

The irony of my nickname for them isn't lost on me. I have been calling them *the chaos twins* since I met them. They were always dressed similarly and still are. The only difference between the two is the blond curls on Mike's head. They have the same features and eyes. Even their ink is similar. I am surprised we haven't thought about the possibility of them being brothers instead of cousins through the years.

Although I guess with all the drama in their families, it does make sense that we never looked into that possibility. Both men tried to forget everything about their past after the fire. I didn't want to remind them of it, so I made sure to never ask.

In a sense, they felt like brothers to me. Even though I know how twisted that sounds, when I am most days balls deep in one of them, from everything we have done in our lifetime, this is not the weirdest thing.

I love them like family, and on paper, we are family as much as we are at heart. Those guys were my salvation when I was lost in depression. I had everything and truly had no reason to be how I was back then. I guess even rich boys can be the black sheep, maybe out of reaction, maybe out of boredom.

I show Liam my phone. He takes it from my hand, reading the report we just got. I can see his lip twitch and his frustration growing. He takes a deep breath before he hands me the phone. I notice his other hand gripping his knife, his knuckles turning white.

He walks fast towards the basement, I don't know if he is going to kill the woman or what, but I follow in silence. *This is not my business,* I keep reminding myself. I stand next to Mike who is now more confused than ever, as Liam passes in front of him and goes down the stairs.

We both watch in silence as he walks to Mary, her eyes meet his, she is clearly afraid when his hand reaches her hair. He strokes her cheek with a look of compassion almost, and then grabs one of her dark locks and cuts it off.

He gives her, his back as he climbs the steps the same way he got down.

"Out!"

He barks the order, and this is so unlike Liam that we are both stunned looking at him. We are forced to take a step back at the same time , when he exits the basement , locking the door behind him.

He grabs me by my shirt and pulls me to follow him and I do, this is not a look I am used to seeing on Liam. I am honestly scared to not follow him at this point. We reach the living room far away from Mike who is still standing in front of the basement with a puzzled look on his face.

He puts the piece of hair in my hand. He grabs one of his curls, and cuts it off with his knife. He places it in my other hand.

"Order a DNA test!"

Another command, and he walks away.

Shit! Okay, I guess I should do that then.

They complain that I am the bossy one, but I am starting to think I am the least dangerous of the group. The chaos twins are truly living up to their name right now.

One of them is a psychotic serial killer, *okay we all are,* and the other one is barking orders and thinking of things I should have. I am too busy worrying about them that the thought of checking with a DNA test did not even cross my mind.

I go to my room and grab two small envelopes, putting the first bundle of hair in one of them and then filling the other one with the second. I label them with their names. Then I take a big envelope and put the small ones in it, and write a letter with my instructions about what to do with it. I put the address of one of our lawyers on the big envelope.

I grab my bike keys and quickly exit the house. *Time to get some answers.*

"I am going out!"

I call as I exit the front door; both of them are too busy to notice.

I need to mail this, but I don't want Mike to know. So, I am going for a ride. With all the drama, it is now morning, and it is the perfect time to do that.

If I am lucky enough, the envelopes will reach the recipient fast enough for us to have an answer in a few days. I am writing an email to the lawyer before I leave the house, explaining the situation the best I can without incriminating myself and the guys.

Liam

The first light of day comes through the window, and I know Jessica's shift starts soon. I was not planning to be there today, but now I feel the need to escape this place, and the reminder of her brings comfort to my troubled mind.

"I am going out."

I announce to Mike, who is now sitting on the floor in front of the basement door.

I am not sure if I should leave him alone, but I need a moment away from this. I decide it is best to take the basement keys with me, so I quickly return and double-lock the door before I take the keys with me. He looks at me but doesn't say a word.

I grab my keys and close the door behind me. I get on my bike and put my helmet over my head, the road is wet from the rain, and the scent of it fills me as I drive to the diner. It is still early, and I know Jessica will be opening right now. I usually avoid arriving this early, making it harder to blend, when no other customers are there, but I need to see her. *I need her more than every other day.*

I arrive just in time to see her trying to open the door, her keys escape her and she curses under her breath.

She hasn't seen me yet, and I am walking behind her.

"Good morning Jessica." I say with a fake smile, after the night I had.

She turns her body around now pressing against mine, I feel her breath brush my lips and the look in her eyes switches from fear to lust in a matter of seconds. She smiles and even though I look down at her, being significantly taller, our faces are on the same level as she looks up, never breaking eye contact.

"Good morning, you are early; we haven't opened yet, but I am sure I can make you a coffee until the cook arrives, maybe see if there is a leftover piece of pie."

She says to me, and I can tell she is not bothered. I am changing her morning routine before the opening.

"There is no problem; I can help you open."

I tell her and take a step forward while she steps back, now her back is against the door. I can't help myself.

I run my fingers on the bare skin of her thigh under her uniform. She takes a deep breath, but isn't one of fear. She doesn't move an inch away from my touch, instead, she puts her hand over mine pressing it softly against her skin and guiding it further up her skirt. She grabs the the fabric of my t-shirt, pulls me closer to her, and I feel her lips of mine.

Her taste invades me and is as sweet as her scent. She always smells of strawberry and vanilla, with some type of flower mixed. A delicious combination that makes me lusting ever more for her.

Her kiss is gentle and passionate at the same time and she moans against my lips as I grab her ass and press her against my now hard cock.

We are still standing in front of the diner's door but none of us care, as I lift her on me and she wraps her legs around my waist.

She grinds on my dick, while we are both fully dressed and I hear someone approach from the back forcing us to break the kiss and her feet to reach the ground.

I take two steps back, putting distance between us. She straightens her uniform and wipes her lips.

"Good morning, Alan."

She greets the cook, and I curse his timing in my head but turn around and offer my hand to the man approaching.

"Hello, I am Liam. I don't believe we have been introduced; sorry for the inconvenience. I had a hard night; your coffee and pie seem to be the best remedy."

I joke, and he shakes my hand, nodding in agreement.

Jessica opens the door, and Alan steps inside first turning the lights on. I see Jessica blush realizing, this is the first time she is hearing my name.

Naughty girl, letting strangers fuck her and kiss her in secret and not even asking for a name.

She turns to me and with a low voice tells me.

"Nice to meet you Liam."

I follow her inside, and she points to my usual booth. I take a seat without saying anything else. *Nice to meet you too baby.*

Nate

I have been away from the house for the last five hours. After I mailed the envelopes, I decided to take some time away and go for a drive. I needed the fresh air to clear my thoughts about the situation. Someone needs to be the voice of reason, and between the three of us, I am the one who is the least emotionally involved.

When I finally step inside the house, there is dead silence. I walk to the basement first. I need to check if the woman is still alive. The moment I reach the door, I see Mike, sleeping on the floor.

He looks broken, and I don't know if Liam had informed him about the details of the situation or if he is simply driving himself crazy, overthinking what it might be, that is happening.

I am fully intending to wake him up, but I need to prioritize. I try turning the door knob, to my surprise I find it locked, but when I reach for the key on the lock like it usually is, I notice it is missing.

I drop to my knees next to Mike, and I place a hand on his shoulder.

"Wake up, buddy."

I say in a low voice as he is waking up from his slumber.

"Nate?"

He questions between sleeping and waking.

"Yes pup, it's me."

I try to reassure him, and I must be doing a good job because he is smiling back at me. He always been a fan of that nickname. I started calling him *puppy*, when we first met. And I only saw a broken boy with a look in his eyes like a lost puppy. That since has changed, but the nickname remains.

"Where is your cousin?" I ask, not sure if I should call him, his *brother*.

"I don't know, he took the key after he locked her in, and left." He tells me, sounding defeated.

I sit next to him and open my arms. He moves closer. I hug him as tight as I can, stroking his hair with one hand, and kissing his head softly.

"I don't know what is happening." He mumbles and I know it is time to tell him.

"Pup I need you to pay attention to what I have to tell you."

He nods and places his head back on my chest, as we sit on the floor.

"During the hunt Mary recognized Liam. This alone seemed weird, but then she told him she is his mother. She also asked about you."

He is now facing me and is sitting upright.

I continue. "He pieced things together and stopped the hunt. When we returned back home, I ordered a background check on her. We found out that she gave birth to twins. We ordered a DNA test, and I am waiting for the results. That's why I was out this morning."

He takes a minute to process the information.

"So, you think she is my mother and Liam's mother."

I nod.

"So, we are brothers but were raised by two different families until the age of ten."

He is reciting the facts we already have, and I nod again.

Before I can say anything else, he gets up and goes to his room; he returns with an extra key for the basement. *Of course, he has a spare key.* Before I have time to question this, I see him open the door.

Mike

I walk into the basement, take a chair, and sit in front of the woman. I remove her gag so she can speak. I have so many questions for her, but I doubt any will be answered. One thing I know for sure, is that she is not going to walk out of this basement alive. But this kill is only mine.

"Hello Mary." I say, my voice cold.

"Are you Mike?"

She asks with hesitation and I nod.

"Where is Amelia? Where is my brother?"

She asks with a tremor in her voice, and continues.

"They will explain everything, please let them explain. You would not believe anything I say, if they don't."

I chuckle.

"They are both dead, I killed them both!"

Her eyes grow dark and tears fill them, but she shakes her head like she is coming to terms with her own fate.

"I will tell you my story if you want to hear it, I know I am probably not going to be walking out of here alive, and I am fully prepared for this. I knew you would come knocking on my door someday. Maybe not in this way, but I always knew I would have to tell you the truth. May as well, if it is the last thing I will do."

She tells me.

I cut her off the restraints and helped her to the couch we have down here, I give her a bottle of water and a blanket. She is cooperating, there is no need for her to suffer at this moment. She thanks me silently with a nod.

"Amelia was my older sister, our brother's favorite, and our parent's pride and joy, She was the good student, the polite one and I was always the failure."

She speaks to me, her eyes focused on the stairs, the entire time. It is clear to me, this is not her first rodeo, she has been in situations like this before.

She watches her back, she doesn't expect to survive. *Smart woman, that's where Liam gets it.* I stay silent, forcing myself to focus on her words.

"She was good to everyone but me, and I was the invisible child no one cared about. Not that this should be an excuse, and it is not. But my parents never cared and my brother always took her side, which made it easy for me to land with the wrong crowd. The misfits of our school. While my brother was the star of the football team, and my sister the popular cheerleader everyone envied. And I... I was the disappointment."

Her words sting not because I feel pity for her, *I don't.* Not because it hurts me she suffered, *it doesn't.* They sting because I know this all too well. I know it from both sides. Liam, Nate, and I were, the people she is describing but that was not always the case. We worked to get to the top and when we got there, we paid them with blood and tears.

She continues telling me her story.

"I was sixteen when I started dating my drug dealer. I was into every type of drug that I could get and spent my time partying. I was already the bad child; there was no need for me to pretend I was better than that. When I found out I was pregnant, I went to Amelia. I asked her to help me. She told my brother and later my parents. All collectively decided it was best for my brother, who was already engaged, to take the baby after I gave birth."

She stops for a moment before she continues.

"I didn't try to fight them as hard as I should have. I didn't try to do anything when the ultrasound showed twins, and they declared that the other baby would be raised by my sister."

I notice a tear falling on her cheek, and I am trying to keep myself distant. I don't need to get attached to this woman. *She is as good as dead, no matter how sad her story is.*

"When I gave birth to you, I tried to change their mind, but they took you away, not even letting me hold you for a second. They shipped me away to private school right after, and I spent every day from that moment, getting my act together. I graduated from school with good grades, went to college, and then later to university. By the time I was done, had met my ex-husband, and was ready to finally meet you, my parents were dead and my siblings refused to return my calls."

She has nothing more to say and she closes her eyes, her head falling against the couch cushion. She drifts to sleep moments later, and I am left there thinking.

I walk out of the basement after what seems like hours. Nate is no longer where I left him. I notice the closed door of his bedroom, and I assume he has gone to bed. I need to feel something, so I make my way into Nate's room. The view of my man sleeping alone takes my breath away. His dark hair slightly falls on his face, and his tan skin is a vast contrast to the ink that decorates it.

My brother and I almost look identical and not half bad. But Nate was always both the brains and the looks, of our little group. His Italian roots are clear, with his tan skin and dark brown hair, his eyes almost appear black in certain lights and honey-brown in others.

But what captivates every part of my existence, is his natural way of dominance. This man could dominate anything and anyone I am sure of it, as sure, I am of my ability to breathe.

I take the space next to him in the bed getting under the covers, as I notice that he is clearly naked. It takes a moment for me to strip of my own clothes, and I get closer to him. He is sleeping on his side with his face planted on the pillow. His hair covers his eyes and I trace the features of his face with my fingers, passing over his lips as I feel him stir against my touch.

I lower my lips to his neck and kiss him, reaching with my hand under the covers. His cock is already hard and I realize he is slowly waking up.

"Pup?"

He murmurs, a mix of statement and a question.

"Yes my love."

I assure him. I wrap my fingers around his dick working him up, kissing and biting his neck at the same time.

I push him to lay on his back, I kiss my way down taking him in my mouth. I need him to take my ability to breathe, make me feel anything other than sorrow and despair.

His finger tangles in my hair and he pushes my face making me tear up as he reaches the back of my throat. I gag and struggle to breathe and he praises me.

"Good boy, keep going."

I obey and lick and nibble at the tip of his cock, before I take him deep in my throat again and again, feeling him tense as he reaches the point of his orgasm, spilling every drop of cum coating my tongue and throat, I savor every drop of him.

"I love you pup."

He tells me. *I love you too.*

Liam

As I arrive at the house, I notice both guys are locked in Nate's room. I take the opportunity to talk to Mary myself. So far I haven't had the chance to get her story on my own, and I might not have another chance.

I move to the basement, finding the door open. Mary hasn't tried to escape, and I walk down the stairs. I reach the mini fridge next to the last step and grab a water bottle offering to her as I approach. She takes it from my hands and I hear her voice as she thanks me.

She sounds broken and sad; I am wondering if I could do anything to help her. If I had refused or claimed she wasn't a good candidate for prey, maybe he would have let it go. Maybe she would have been spared. Thinking more about this, I am convincing myself that he wouldn't possibly let it go. Nate and I did everything in our power to change his mind.

"Mary, we haven't been introduced formally. I am Liam."

I tell her, and she nods. I observe her as she takes a deep breath, and her eyes find mine. She smiles, a motherly smile that I have so missed seeing on my own mother.

"You were so small when you were born." She tells me, and I chuckle.

She continues on her own. It looks like I don't need to say anything else; she is about to share everything she is willing to on her own.

"Mike was born first. He didn't stop crying from the moment he got out until they took him away, but you came out right after and barely cried. I thought something was wrong with you. They kept you away, and even though I couldn't see, I heard whispers as they tried to help you. Eventually, I heard your first cry, but even that was so soft and low in volume that you would not believe it came from a newborn."

She almost sounds like a proud mother. It would fool me if I didn't know better.

She then looks at me; her eyes have another form of darkness, One I almost recognize. Her words now are almost above a whisper, almost like she is hesitating, but it feels like this is something important.

"I told this to Mike already, but I want you to know as well. I never wanted to let you go; I tried. I fought to keep you. But they wouldn't have it."

Tears are falling from her eyes, and I am not sure how to react. I had so many things to tell her, and at this moment, I have nothing. I don't wish to interrogate this woman anymore. I don't want to ask her about her reasons for leaving us. I don't even care that she did it.

Even though we have been through hell, we did come out okay in the end. We survived, and it is safe to say we made our share of mistakes along the way. We are not entitled to judgment for this poor woman.

I have returned to the house for at least an hour. When Mike finally enters the living room, where I am sitting in my usual spot by the window. I look at Mike as he gets comfortable on the couch, and even though I want him to take his time before we talk about this, I can't wait.

Nate texted me; he told me everything we know so far, and the lawyer informed me with a lengthy call that the DNA results, even though they would be useful, are not that important. He was able to find evidence by contacting my family's lawyer. The adoption papers and our original birth certificates, which he was able to find, both list Mary as the mother.

"I talked to the lawyer."

I say, breaking the silence, in need of sharing this with him. I am purposely avoiding letting him know about my conversation with Mary.

"Okay." He simply replies.

I am not sure I like this side of him.

"We are still waiting for the DNA results, but he looked into the case himself and found our original birth certificates, along with adoption papers. Both of them have listed Mary as our birth mother."

He looks puzzled, and then he speaks, his words barely a sound.

"I always thought of you as my brother; this changes nothing."

I smile at his statement. *You were always my brother, Mike.*

"I will always be by your side, but we have to decide on this woman's fate. I know you, and I am not delusional enough to believe she will be spared." I tell him.

He takes a moment too long, lost in his own mind before he speaks.

"Look, I would love to spare her, but you are right; this is not something I am capable of doing. She told me her story while you were gone. A sad one indeed. She was only a child herself when everything happened."

He seems to have some sense of remorse in his voice regarding his decision, but I know for a fact this won't change a thing.

But when it comes to this man, it is progress. He has killed so many people on his way out of hell, with only feeling an ounce of remorse. But now he can understand the weight of his decision, this might be the only positive thing we will get from her death. The events won't change, but my brother might face a glimpse of hope for redemption.

"Whatever you decide to do, I will be by your side."

I tell him finally, and without saying anything else I walk to my room. I will be thinking more clearly after some sleep, and that's what I intend to do, as I close the door behind me.

Mike,
The night of the accident

I am sitting next to Lena in the back seat of my stepfather's car. We are driving for a family pizza night in town, but I know we will never make it. I messed up the brakes of the car right before we started; I didn't know Lena would join us, though.

She is usually doing something else on those nights, this girl has put, so much on her schedule. She is incredibly smart and is trying to get into a good college. Already has her goals and dreams set, working towards them with everything she has.

I reach her side and try to lower her window again. She smacks my hand.

"Stop it." She tells me.

"I just need more air." I respond defeated. *Please let me save you.*

I have tried to lower her window three times by now, and we are almost at the bridge. I know he will have to press the brake pedal when we get there to slow down while passing the bridge. I was counting on taking that route and that with the rain and the messed up brakes, he will lose control.

I made sure not to not wear my seat belt even though my mother told me to do so multiple times. I ignored her. I tried to convince Lena to not put on hers, but she ignored me instead.

The rain is pouring like crazy, and the car windows are getting fogged. We start going onto the bridge, and as I predicted, my stepfather tries to hit the brake.

The car screeches as the tires grind on the slippery road, but it doesn't stop. He tries again and again. I can see him getting mad and trying to keep hold of the car as the tires slip on the wet road at full speed. He fails.

I decide that there is nothing I can do right now but complete what I started. I stand on my seat, reaching over to the driver's seat.I push the steering wheel, turning the car toward the edge of the bridge.

I fall back and cover Lena with my body as the car falls into the lake. Everyone struggles, and my father is furious.

My mother says something I can't hear with all the screaming coming next to me. I see him trying to find something to break the windows on his side. This man only cares about himself and no one else. The car is filling with water quickly from my open window, I see everyone trying to unbuckle their seat belts, but no one is breaking free.

I am trying to help my sister, but it is pointless. I am looking for something to cut the seat belt. I made sure to throw the knife, I used for the brakes, so my father couldn't use it to cut his or my mother's.

I am holding my breath and now the car is almost reaching the bottom of the lake, I need to act quickly or I will run out of air. I pull her seat belt along with her, and I try to help her get under it but it is too tight. The belt is now locked in place. *This is my fault.*

It is not long before I come to the conclusion, I won't be able to set her free. I need to get myself out of this car, before I am drowning with them. I don't wish to let them ruin my life more than they already did.

I push my body out of the window, I am running out of air. I am trying to swim to the surface fast. I don't manage to do that. I am losing cautiousness. As my eyes close shut, I see a figure swimming towards the car, and I hope in my delusional state that, whoever it is will help my sister.

Next thing I know I am on the side of the road and a guy is performing CPR on me. I cough the water in my lungs, and try to look around, searching for my sister. He must have tried to get her out. He couldn't have left her behind.

"Where is Lena?"

I ask, but he shakes his head.

"I am sorry I tried to get the girl out but I couldn't. Your parents were already dead by the time I reached the car, and she had a faint pulse. They are trying to retrieve the bodies now."

My eyes fall to the ground, I am responsible for this. This is all my fault. I sacrificed her life to end my nightmare yet, I am not sure I regret it as much as I should.

I never intended for her to get hurt. I only needed to stop the pain, the suffering, the torment. I wanted to make sure they won't touch me again.

I needed to be sure they wouldn't touch her. She wasn't his type. He never touched his precious daughter, but that could easily change.

Lena was my stepfather's daughter; they joined our family when I was three. Lena was ten. She was a small girl, and most people thought we were about the same age the older I got. Now at the age of ten, I am as tall as her.

I never knew my biological father, and he adopted me right away.

My mother had told me countless times how my biological father died while she was pregnant with me. He was happy to meet me, according to her story, but he never got to.

What always troubled me is that none of the stories matched; the only thing that matched was the fact that he died in every single one, but the way was different. At first, she was claiming a tragic accident; then she moved to more horrific stories, like that he got murdered.

I never knew the truth. I guess now I will never know. Something tells me, though, that there is more to that story, I am thinking to myself, I should have done more to figure it out, before I ended their lives.

I am waiting on the side of the road next to a police car, for the social worker that will be assigned to my case. They are taking me to a foster home for a few days, until they can locate the closest family member to assign me to.

I already know they will be handing me over to Liam's father. My grandparents are dead and his family lives in the same town as mine. I would not have to change schools and lose friends. This is something that they look for, when they place a child in a new home. They are trying to ensure that their life will be less interrupted as possible. Especially when that child has suffered the loss of both parents.

To the government and social workers, I am an innocent child who needs to be protected. I am someone they need to care for; they need to provide If only they knew, I would be going to a much different prison than the one they will send me now.

Liam's family home is as good as one, though. My uncle is as bad as my stepfather. The only difference is he likes to beat them with his belt instead of sneaking into their rooms at night. That I can take. I can figure out how to get both myself and my cousin out of his house as soon as possible.

I already have a plan but it needs to be worked out. I am not staying there longer than I have to. The first opportunity I get to take the bastard out or set him straight, I am taking it.

I walk to the edge of the bridge, where the railing is broken from the car falling against it. I look down, and I open my hand. I look at the bracelet Lena gave me a year ago. It has black beads and the letter "L" hanging from it. The matching one with pink beads and the letter "M" is on her wrist.

I look back at the ambulance they are putting her body in now, and I toss the black bracelet into the water. *Rest in peace Lena, I never wanted you to join them.*

Nate

This situation we have gotten ourselves into is more messed up than usual. I am holding my man by force to not break in pieces. He is about to start spiraling, any moment now, and I am fully aware that the woman in our basement won't survive this.

Sadly until the chaos twins do something about her, it is my responsibility to care for her needs. I am standing in the kitchen cooking, while Liam is somewhere, that no one knows again and Mike is lost in his thoughts sitting on the living room's couch.

In all honesty, I do prefer him sitting on his ass to causing us more trouble than we can afford at the moment. The food is almost done. I will be the first to admit that I am not the best cook, but plain pasta with some cheese on it will be the best this woman will get from us. Still better than letting her starve like Liam proposed or killing her on the spot like Mike wanted.

I have grown up with money, and that is not a secret. The boys joined my family in the last year of high school, and my parents were more than happy to legally adopt them.

I used to be a troubled one myself. I almost dropped out a couple of times until I met the guys in my senior year. My parents paid for universities and colleges for all three of us, and when the time came, we all got a share of the family company.

Even though we all now collectively own my family's fortune, I am the one controlling everything. I never cared that my parents made sure to provide for the twins, though. I wouldn't have it any other way.

They deserve everything we had to offer them. Those men had so much pain early in life, and I couldn't relate to that, but I always wished to protect them.

I had a good childhood: loving parents, winters in snowy resorts, and summers in exotic destinations. I have driven a nice car since I got my license. I always had the luxury of being dressed in the finest clothes and had everything I ever wanted.

My parents provided me with an education, kept me well-dressed and fed, and were always there to celebrate every accomplishment I ever achieved.

I had it easy in comparison to the twins. This is why now I am the one to take care of their mother, being held captive in our house. Because I know these men would do the same, in a heartbeat, if things were different.

I owe this woman the decency of her last moments to be half okay, I think while heading to the basement with a plate of pasta and a bottle of water.

I find the woman curled up on the basement couch. And from what Liam and Mike have told me, this is the spot she has been in since we got back after chasing her through the maze.

She looks broken, and part of this is as much of my responsibility as theirs. Her eyes meet mine and then fall on the plate of pasta. She shakes her head.

"I am not hungry."

She tells me and turns her head to the other side facing the wall. *We will be your downfall Mary and for that I am sorry.*

Mike

Nate is trying to feed Mary, who is refusing to eat, knowing well, this is her last moments alive. I honestly don't know why he bothers, she will be dead soon. We never had any women captive, usually ending the hunt with blood but this situation is different. Smart woman, I will give her that.

She is using pity to her advantage trying to get to whoever she can, in hopes to let her go. I don't know where Liam is and at this time, I have no intention of poking into his business. My brother likes his secrets, and I need him to be able to cope.

I already know I will end Mary's life tonight. I also know the men in my life will try to save her out of fear of what killing my mother all over again, will do to me. I have made up my mind on how to do it, killing time until the night comes.

Nate enters the living room, and drops the plate he is holding on the coffee table.

"She did not touch the food again." He claims.

I chuckle at the thought. My boyfriend is struggling to take care of a soon to be dead woman.

"I am guessing that being captive in a basement can reduce appetite."

I point out, with a serious tone. Then start laughing as the idea of how messed up the situation is crosses my mind.

he gives me an annoyed look, and I laugh louder.

He steps closer, taking my face in his hands, pushing, my chin up.

"Pup, you are being a brat. That is not polite."

He teases, brushing his finger against my lips, and I lick it without breaking eye contact. I can sense the tension crackling between us, a playful game of dominance and submission.

He grabs me by my throat and pushes me against the couch, towering my body with his.

"You know better pup." He warns and I nod.

My hand falls against his hard length over his jeans, and I unbutton his pants, eager to have a taste of him.

When his cock is free, I wrap my fist around it, stroking him while I take his lips with mine. He moans against my mouth, and I pick up my pace. I am not usually the one to take charge, and in a way, I don't. But that little sense of power that he will allow me in this moment is much needed.

He pushes my head down.

"Be a good boy and suck my cock pup."

His voice filled with lust and passion. I obey his command and take him in my mouth. He grabs a fist full of hair and begins to fuck my mouth hard.

Tears stain my cheeks, and I am gasping for air only making him moan harder and go faster. I wouldn't have it any other way. He is pumping in and out and I stick my tongue out ready for him, to give me that taste I crave.

A growl escapes him as he comes inside my mouth and I savor every drop of him like a starving man.

"Good boy." He praises me and leans to kiss my lips softly.

He takes the seat by my side and I curl next to him, his arms wrapped around me. My own piece of heaven right here, in this man's arms. I can't let anything get to me as long as he is around. He is my safe place, my heart, and my soul.

Liam

By the time I wake up, both guys have fallen asleep on the couch. Their naked bodies are tangled in a chaos of limbs. Even though I love my brother and my friend to death, this is a little more than I would like to see of them.

I take a seat in the armchair next to the couch and the movement must have woken them up, as Nate is giving me a sleepy look.

"Hey there." I say cheerfully.

My morning with Jess having a clear impact on my mood still. Mike mumbles something I can't quite hear, and Nate stretches before he wraps his arms around my brother again bringing him closer.

The view of the two of them leads me to a path of thoughts and desires, I don't have the courage to admit to myself. I wonder about all the possibilities, Jessica and I would have, if I had chosen a different path in life. *If only.*

Nate

The chaos twins have been chatting about something upstairs, and I have found myself in a quest for answers. I need to know more of this woman's story before I let blood spill under my roof.

As my feet reach the last step, I see her sitting straight. She is not tied up anymore, but is still a captive in every sense.

She is free to use the bathroom that we have down here, and I am bringing her food every few hours, but other than that she is still a prisoner.

"Mary, I would like to ask you some questions."

I start telling her and she nods.

"I know you told Mike your story."

she nods again.

"But I want to know what happened to you, after the boys lost their families. Mike told me you claimed to not know, but there are multiple news stories on the internet, and it was a thing on the media for a while after. Conspiracy stories about how the boys killed both families had been circling the internet for years after their deaths."

She takes a breath and accepts defeat.

"I knew they were dead. I learned the news about a week after it happened."

She explains and now I am starting to get mad, but I need to contain myself.

I take the seat next to her and I continue talking, following the thread of what I have been weaving in my mind since we arrived back home, with her as our captive. Something doesn't fit, and I need to know how right or wrong I am.

"So, even though you knew and you claim that your parents forced you to give your babies to your brother and sister, you still did nothing after their passing to get your kids back."

I lay my observation and she nods again.

"Your parents though, had been dead for a while at this point. Correct?"

She stays quiet.

"From what I have learned about you, when the accidents occurred, you were already married and had enough money to support your two sons, if needed."

She nods again and before I continue she opens her lips to say something but hesitates. I stay silent giving her time.

Her whole body language changes and now her voice lacks fear. It's cold as ice.

"I never wanted them. I knew my family would give them to my siblings. That's why I went to my sister for help."

I huff knowing well that, I was right.

"So you lied to your kids even though you know this is the end for you. Do you know what happened to them?"

I ask her.

She shakes her head.

"Liam bled every day under your brother's belt, and your sister looked the other way when her husband found himself being satisfied by fucking an eight-year-old Mike every night."

Her face twitches like she is in pain, and I continue.

"The rumors though, are indeed true. The twins are responsible for the death of all of them".

I take a deep breath, needing a moment.

"Some were innocent and some well deserving, but when you are in pain your actions are not that well calculated. They never intended to kill their siblings or Liam's mother. She had done everything in her power to protect them, but she was a victim herself. I know he is considering her as his mother, even though you gave birth to him."

She doesn't talk and I get up to leave, but turn to say one more thing to her.

"I hope you rot in hell, Mary. For every ounce of pain, you cost these men."

With that I leave her, knowing well, it won't be long before she ends up dead. I needed to know, if her death would be in vain or not. Now I do.

Mike

Liam is talking about a movie or a TV show, and I am not listening to any of this. My focus is on the sneaky man who just left my side and walked to the basement. I am not sure what he is doing, but he would have said something if he were going to just check on her. I am not too worried; he is not the murdery type unless it is part of the game.

"You know it is a really good movie." Liam tells me, and I nod. *Sure it is, buddy.*

"This actor is amazing; he has done so many good films that it is ridiculous he is not famous yet." He continues.

Yes, Liam, I am sure he is really talented; shut the fuck up now, I need to know what Nate is doing.

I don't say this, though; I nod instead, agreeing with him.

"Yes, I am sure he will be famous soon; we should watch a film of his."

He gets excited .

"Yeah, let me pull up something on my laptop."

He gets up to go grab his laptop, and I take the opportunity to check on my man. I don't like things being out of my control. I peek through the basement door, and it seems like I am lucky enough to be unnoticed.

They are just talking, and I can't process this before I hear Liam's steps from the other side, approaching the living room.

I run back and flop on the couch, breathless, trying to calm myself as he comes and sits on the floor next to my feet.

He puts a film on, and we spend the next hour watching a horror movie. It is really bad quality, in my opinion, but my brother reacts like it is the best thing he has seen in forever. He always liked bad horror films, and I always despised them. I do love seeing him smile and laugh, though, so I am watching it with him while my mind is still on the sneaky guy in our basement, talking to a woman he shouldn't.

Nate comes back, and it is at least an hour and something later. He sits next to me and hangs an arm over my shoulder, pulling me onto his body. I lean back on him, pretending everything is okay, not wanting to ruin the first normal evening we are having in what seems like forever.

Nate,

Seventeen years old

I am late and I have no idea where I am going. I am trying to find my way through this labyrinth of a high school for an hour now. I am pretty sure I have the wrong map or something. Nothing is where it should be.

I spot a class where the door is still open. It is the right number. I am not sure if it is the right building. At this point, I will risk it. I enter and I see an empty seat at the back. I quickly walk over and sit down.

The guy next to me is looking at me with concern; he almost seems mad. I am about to say something, but then I hear another guy from the front, picking on the guy in front of the angry one.

The boy looks broken; he is really thin, and I am wondering if he is even being fed. He looks identical to the angry guy but almost not; both of them are too skinny for their height. He has blonde hair and his eyes have a gloom of sorrow in them.

The angry guy gets up.

"Do you want to repeat that, Alex?"

He questions the other guy, *Alex,* who is now walking fast, approaching us. His fist is curled, and he is about to punch the angry guy when I get up and punch him first.

"What the hell!"

He screams as his finger touches the blood coming from his nose and I smirk. I finally see I am in the wrong class; everyone looks younger, so I get my bag and turn to the angry guy.

"Sorry about that, I am pretty sure you would love a punch, to start your morning. I am Nate, see you around." I tell him and wink, before I turn my back to him.

The skinny blonde boy approaches me as I get out of the door. He pulls me to the side, hiding me from the view of the class.

"I am Mike, thank you for that. The one who looks like me but angrier is Liam."

I smile and swipe a strand of his hair out of his face.

"Nice to meet you, Mike."

I tell him, and he smiles back at me. *His smile is the best thing that happened today.*

I don't know what it is, but I feel like I will be seeing a lot of those two. They look like trouble, and I am supposed to stay out of that. They moved me schools for the third time this year because of all the fights I was getting into.

Here I am, starting my first day in the wrong class by punching a random dude for the honor of a skinny guy, who I am pretty sure is straight. *Great job, Nate.*

Mike

It is the middle of the night, and I pull myself under Nate's sleeping body, careful not to make a sound, as both my boyfriend and my brother are sleeping like the dead in our living room.

Liam is curled up in the armchair, and from the look of it, I know he must be really uncomfortable. He doesn't seem to have the energy to wake up, let alone to go up to his room.

I walk into my room to retrieve my knife, and move quickly to the basement. Where Mary is sleeping on the couch. There is a lock on the basement's door but other than that, we did nothing to restrain her, giving her free roam to the basement, for as long as we have been holding her captive.

I take a few steps and she stirs in her sleep, as I bring my knife to her throat. She jolts awake and a gasp leaves her lips.

"I am sorry *Mother,* but it will benefit no one if you live, you know too much, you did too much."

I say before I slit her throat.

I watch her from above choking on her own blood. She is awake now, her eyes are wide and blood is spilling from her throat and mouth.

She is gagging and gasping for air, as I watch her spark of life leave her eyes. She falls limp against my arms.

A sense of calmness fills me, and my demons are finally satisfied. I carry her lifeless body up the stairs, out of the back door in our backyard placing it on the ground. I take the shovel from the shed and start digging.

The ground is moist from all the rain and easy to dig in, it doesn't take me long to have a deep enough hole for her.

I push her body in without one ounce of remorse, I start covering her up. When I am finished, I spit on the ground *Rot in hell, Mother.*

I know I should feel something other than hate and anger. I have really tried, I wanted to spare her life for my brother.

I know this pains him. All this death around us, breaks pieces of him one by one. I am starting to feel like he is a ghost. He is not talking much, barely eats, and disappears for hours at a time. He has always been a loner and that hasn't been much of a concern until now.

But the guy learned, that his biological mother let him be raised by a monster, and did nothing. He didn't even react. It is like the information barely touched him. This is not like Liam.

I know I didn't handle it too well myself, but this reaction is expected of me. Like, my track of kills has shown, I tend to overreact and get a little too bloodthirsty. Liam though, bottles things up, but he never shuts us completely out.

I walk into the house, and it is like I summoned the guy with my thoughts, as he is now sitting with his arms crossed, leaning on the wall, right behind the door. He looks at me and I give him a smirk.

"Mommy dearest is dead."

I announce.

He starts following me as I walk to my room leaving traces of mud on the carpet.

"I said, I will support you! You couldn't wait to do it with me? Or let me do it instead?"

He questions .

"All this blood on your hands Mike. You could share the pain for once!"

He is angry.

"Liam you can't handle it, and you know it. You haven't even killed a woman, in all the years of hunting them."

I respond and his eyes fall to the ground.

"We have been hunting women since college, not once you had put your knife even close to them. You live for the hunts, you are more than happy to get rid of the evidence and that makes you part of the team as much as any of us, but you don't kill!"

He looks like I pulled the carpet under his feet.

"Maybe you are right. I wanted to be there for you at least" He admits.

"I love you for that. You know I do."

I tell him in return and push him slightly to step out of my room, closing the door behind me. *Goodnight brother.*

I walk to the bathroom and remove my clothes. I search in the cabinet under my sink for a plastic bag. I open the black trash bag, and set the clothes inside. They are ruined for good. Bummer too; this t-shirt was one of my favorites.

I remove the "L" pendant I wear around my neck, setting it on the counter. I lean into the shower and turn it on. I clean my face at the sink, removing blood stains with a towel, and throw it in the bag with my clothes, before I step into the shower.

I stand under the hot stream, the water washes the blood off my hair, and I make sure to clean it well, washing it twice.

Maybe I should dye it red, that would hide blood stains more easily. I chuckle at the thought.

The water has turned cold and I turn it off, stepping out of the shower I wrap a towel around myself and walk to my bed. I don't bother to get dressed, I haven't slept with clothes on since I was living at Nate's house, and he would sneak at night in my room or I would sneak into his.

Liam

He killed her. It should not be a shock to me. We all knew it would happen. The thoughts torment me as I drive to Jess's house. All I want is to see her, but I know I shouldn't invade her personal space, especially when she's unaware of my knowledge of her house's location. Even though I have been doing this for the past few weeks.

The need to feel anything other than the sadness I'm currently experiencing, is overwhelming. It's a feeling I've never thought I'd experience again. I park my motorcycle behind a tree, blocking Jessica's view from her window as I walk through the backyard, trying to convince myself not to climb up to her bedroom.

It's a moment too long, before I realize I'm halfway up. I finish the remaining distance, stepping onto the small balcony. It's dark inside, but when I try to open the window, I'm not surprised to find, it opens for me.

I step inside and immediately notice the sleeping form on her bed, her bare skin peeking out from under the covers, her hair covering her beautiful features.

I take a step closer and lift the covers of her naked sleeping body, shedding my own clothes. I get in bed behind her and press my body against hers. She jolts awake and I can feel her tense against my touch, as I run my fingers on her side, gripping her ass firmly.

"It's me." I whisper to her, not sure, if she will know who is the *me* I am referring to but she surprises me when she calls my name.

"Liam?"

Her voice full of disbelief.

"Yes sweetheart."

I reassure her and she relaxes against my body. I press my hard cock against her ass, and she gasps. I reach with one hand between her legs and press two fingers inside her. I kiss and nibble on her neck softly. She moans, her body reacting to my touch and I keep fucking her faster with my fingers.

"Please, Liam."

she begs and I pick up my pace going faster, harder. Her sweet moans feel the room as her pussy spasm around my fingers.

Before she has time to fully come down from her orgasm, I flip her on the bed, her breasts push against the mattress. I lift her ass and bring my lips against her sweet pussy.

The moment my tongue touches her clit, her body shakes against the sensation, and I resume where I have left, licking her and fucking her with two fingers inside her. It doesn't take long before a second orgasm washes over her, and my name slips of her lips.

"Liam."

I smile, and I get on my knees, on the bed. I rub my cock on her clit ,"Good girl" I praise, before I enter her with a hard thrust.

She gasps trying to adjust to my size. I allow her a moment, trailing a path of kisses on her back praising her .

"You doing so good for me."

When I feel her body slowly relax again I start moving, with slow and passionate moves, our moans now mixing. I feel myself quickly going over the edge, her tight pussy is milking my cock, coming around it all over again. I can't wait to fill her up with my own cum. I spill inside her, while she is still coming out of her orgasm, a sweet moan escapes her lips.

We fall against the mattress breathless, and I pull her in my arms not wanting to leave her yet.

"You are the only one, I can think of lately."

I whisper, and it is mostly true. She is quickly falling asleep. Her body is now spent and satisfied. It is not long before I, myself follow her.

Jessica

The first light of day, comes through my bedroom window. I am in the arms of the man, who has captivated every living moment of my life since I met him.

I would usually be more worried about a stranger breaking into my house, in the middle of the night, but Liam has a way of making me feel safe, in situations I really shouldn't. He has been the only desire I have had, since he stepped into the diner during my shift, almost a month ago now.

At first, he was only the guy that watched me work. He wouldn't come close enough or talk to me for a long time. Then he suddenly changed. I have been catching myself wishing for him to be around more and more.

He has brought a sense of safety and danger, both at the same time, into my life that I welcome. He makes me feel alive and loved when everyone else, until now, made me feel the opposite.

A nice change to feel wanted for once. To feel like someone would do anything for you. Even though he hasn't said anything of such nature to me. I have a feeling that he would do great things for me. *In a sense, I would do anything for him too.*

Nate

I am usually not the stalking my friends type, but those idiots have been behaving like heathens. One of them murders women and puts them in our backyard like it's another Sunday, and the other one apparently is now is stalking them, breaking into their homes for a little action.

I pace in the stranger woman's backyard as I think about what to do, to control the men in my life. I love them to death, but I don't mean my death. They need to stop behaving like wild animals.

I take my motorcycle and drive back to the house, swiftly getting inside. I go straight to Mike's bedroom.

"Wake up, your brother is breaking entry now, just to get some pussy."

I announce as I enter. Mike that has already been awake it seems, chuckles.

"Well it is about time, he got some action."

He teases and I frown.

"Relax my love. We can deal with this in a fun way, no need to be a dick about it."

He explains as he pulls me in bed, helping me out of my clothes. I relax against his touch as he kisses his way from my neck to my cock. I am already getting hard, he takes me in his mouth and a moan escapes me. *Fuck this man knows how to shut me up.*

"You are using your lips to shut me up."

He takes me deeper in response.

" Fuck." I growl "Good boy keep going."

My cock slips in and out of his mouth each time reaching a little deeper. He nibbles at the tip before he takes me all the way down again, reaching the back of his throat. I am pounding and grabbing the sheets not able to hold for much longer.

" I am going to come."

I warn him and he picks up his pace even more, making it so hard for me to hold from spilling down his throat. And that's exactly what I do.

My cum covers his tongue and spills out of his mouth. He turns his head up and looks at me, wiping a small string of it dripping down his lip.

" Feeling better?"

He asks, and I laugh.

"Much better." I tell him.

He curls up on my side, and I hug him tight. "Thank you, pup."

He smiles.

"No problem, at your service, Sir." His voice is full of playfulness, a side of Mike I have missed.

It is not long before we are both asleep. In his arms is the only way I can get any sleep. He has always been the one to bring a sense of safety into my life, even before we started killing people for sport.

He is the love of my life, and even though I don't tell him, I am pretty sure he knows. I would bet good money he even feels the same.

I am standing in the kitchen with a cup in my hand full of coffee that I haven't touched and is now is getting cold. Mike is sitting on the counter next to me when Liam enters through the kitchen door that leads to the backyard. *The bastard thinks he can sneak in.*

I am ready to say something, but Mike speaks first.

"Sneaking in, are we?"

We both know where he was, but he doesn't need to know we do.

"Killed any mothers lately?"

Liam responds, *oh he is pissed about Mommy.*

"Nope, just the bitch that gave us away."

Mike responds in all honesty, and I am thinking right now that I should really reconsider my friendships.

"Oh come on you can't tell me you are sad about it. We both knew I would kill her." He adds.

"I am not sad. However, I am pissed. Yes, I knew she would die, but I was hoping this time, you would have let me be a part of it. Her actions had caused me as much pain."

Okay I will give him that, he does have a point.

"Well, you would have done nothing about it, even if I had let you. You love the chase, but spilling blood is not your thing Liam."

Mike is not wrong either.

"You are probably right." Liam finally admits. *I agree.*

"I am sorry, I acted without you."

Mike apologizes, even though we all know, he doesn't mean it. *Look at my man, trying to play nice.*

"I forgive you."

Liam accepts it in return. *That's a good sign, he is letting it go.*

"Friends again? Great. Now boys, what's next?"

I finally speak, trying to change the subject. *Take the bait, Liam.* We have already reached the five kills for this town. We need to move.

"I think we should stay for another week."

Liam tells us and he walks out of the room.

I turn to Mike and he is now looking at me with a well-known look on his face.

"We need to figure out how serious this thing between them is."

He tells me. *I agree.*

He kisses me in a failed attempt to calm me down, my lips part for him instantly.

"Pup you can't keep distracting me with sex."

He smirks. "Why not? It is clearly working. You are hard already!"

His fingertips brush against my hard cock, over my pants.

"That is unrelated." I try to argue.

"You need to stop worrying so much," he whispers and kisses my neck.

"Turn around."

I order him and he does like the good boy, I know he is.

"Remove your pants and boxers." One more command for him to follow. *Good boy.*

"Part your legs for me and bend over the counter." I give him another one.

"Yes sir."

He replies as he does what he is told. I open one of the cabinets, we stock extra products of our essentials, and I grab a bottle of lube. I squirt some on my fingers and I push two inside his ass pushing some lube inside, as I prep him.

"Fuck keep going."

He begs, and I fuck him with my fingers faster. I take the lube bottle again and pour a generous amount on my cock stroking it. I enter him with a hard thrust, and he pushes against me, to take me deeper, moaning with every thrust as I fuck him.

He is stroking himself while I fuck him, and I order him once more .

"Be a good boy and come for me."

He picks ups his pace, and it is not long before he is spilling his release on the kitchen floor.

"Good boy." I praise.

"On your knees." Another order as I pull out of him.

He gets on his knees and turns to face me.

"Open your mouth boy."

I demand. I am stroking myself ready to reach my own orgasm. He opens his mouth, his eyes find mine, right in time for my cum to spill all over his tongue and face.

"Fuck you look so pretty on your knees with my cum all over your face pup."

I say, as I reach for a towel, handing it to him to clean himself.

Mike

We are sitting in a rental car watching a diner, at the center of the town. The local church is right down the street, and on a Sunday morning, the diner is packed with the crowd, after the morning service.

Liam is sitting in a booth alone, sipping on a cup of coffee. He observes the brunette woman serving customers, like she is the most amazing creature.

She is absolutely stunning, that I can admit. I see why my brother is obsessed with her. I also can see why he hasn't shared his latest find. He is afraid she will end up playing our little game.

"He has been here every day for the past week." Nate points out.

"I know. I have been in the same car as you, watching him for the past week, Nate."

He is not happy; this is something he can't control. Nate doesn't appreciate things that he cannot control.

"I am sure he has a reason for not telling us about her."

I try to defend my brother. Yeah, *he does; it is called, 'I don't want my girlfriend to end up slaughtered by you heathens.'* I choose to not share this thought with my clearly irritated boyfriend.

"I am sure he does."

He replies, defeated, and I can tell he is bottling up some serious feelings.

Nate always dealt with his emotions by not dealing with them. I deal with them by killing people, and Liam is spiraling through eternity or bottling them up. *At least we are all fucked up together.*

"Where did he go?" Nate yells.

I try to search for Liam in the crowded restaurant catching a glimpse of him, as he follows the brunette in the back.

"Let's try the back."

I propose and we both exit the car at the same time. We walk to the back side of the diner, but stop at our feet, when we hear a moan.

"You gotta be kidding me!"

Nate says, and I place my hand over his lips, in an attempt to keep him quiet.

"He is fucking her in the middle of the day, in the back of a diner!"

He declares keeping his voice low this time, like the noises coming from this woman, wasn't enough of a statement.

"Maybe he has suffered a brain injury we don't know about recently, and it makes him act crazy."

I say in return, and now Nate is glaring at me, like his eyes will shoot laser at any minute.

"Calm down, I am not the one fucking her."

I joke but he is in no mood to appreciate it.

"That asshole will get us caught!"

He says again, his voice rising, and I gesture to him to keep it down.

"We need to leave this town." He mumbles.

"Or... and hear me out... We can kidnap her, and put her in the maze."

I counter propose. He pauses for a second before agreeing with me.

"That might work." *Good, finally we will have some fun.*

"Maybe we should stop watching my brother fuck his girl."

I point and he looks confused, I am pulling him back to the car.

"Come on big guy, time to get you back in the car."

I am physically dragging him back to the car at this point. When we reach the car, I open the passenger's seat and push him in.

"Stay!" I tell him and he frowns.

I circle the car and get in the driver's seat.

"How are you doing buddy?"

He is basically one step away from smoke coming out of his ears.

I start the car before I watch Nate burst into that diner, and Liam being dragged into the car by his hair.

Nate

He will get us all caught or killed for a woman. I get the need to get your dick wet like the next guy but, Jesus this is not the best way to go about it. Especially when you are traveling through the country, killing women. He is usually the one thinking of details to not get us caught. This is so out of character for my friend.

We had been at the house for two hours when he finally arrived.

He is now sitting on the floor of our living room, chatting with Mike about a TV show or something with his dog sleeping next to him while he pets him. I am really trying to ignore the situation and failing.

It is the only thing in my mind right now. We need to figure out a plan but in the meantime, I have to get out of here.

"I am going for a drive."

I announce and grab my keys.

Both men nod and go back to their conversation.

I take my bike for a quick drive to clear my head. *Maybe things will be fine. He will have his fun and move on.*

Liam

It has been a few days since I went to see Jessica; the feeling of being watched the other day keeps coming to mind. I suspect they know, but I can't be sure until I have some evidence. I am just playing it safe until then.

Nate has been irritated about something barely speaking to me. Mike on the other hand is being really chatty about everything, in a great mood for someone who killed his biological mother, a week ago.

With Mary, we have reached the limit. I know we should be moving. Part of me wants to indulge in the thought of Jessica joining us, but I know she would never agree.

She would probably be terrified if she knew what I am. If she knew how much pain and suffering, we have caused in the past few years. I am pretty sure, she has seen her fair share of darkness, but nothing can compare with what we are.

I am obsessed with that woman, I have no idea why. She is beautiful, sure. That alone doesn't really explain why I am willing to go behind everyone's back in order to steal a few moments with her.

I am risking everything by getting close to her. We are avoiding getting caught by remaining unseen. I can usually achieve that while still having my usual routine of coffee and people-watching in the various diners. I am pretty sure, though, getting close with the waitress in a small town like this is a recipe for disaster.

It won't be long before someone notices me, rumors will start, and people will gossip. When we leave eventually and they discover the first body or make a connection about the five women vanishing through thin air. They might think about the tall guy with dark hair, that was fucking the waitress on her break.

I need to stop seeing her, but I am pretty sure this is beyond my powers. She is addictive in every sense. She will be the one to send me to hell. I am fully aware of it, yet I still can't seem to stay away.

Nate

We have been stalking this fool for days now. He tells us he is going out with no explanation, and the moment he starts his bike, we are both out of the door and down the road, where the rental car is parked.

I did put a tracker on his bike. It was the most reasonable way to track him, Mike suggested putting it in his neck instead. For a moment, I will admit, I did entertain the idea. This man has taken me out of my clothes, and it is not the fun way his brother does it.

This will be bad for all of us, when we leave and someone suspects the mysterious dude, Jessica was sneaking around with for the murders. He must know that. He can't be that stupid.

"I was meaning to talk to you about something."

I start in an attempt to take my mind out of the guy we are stalking and his whore.

"Yeah? What's that?"

Mike responds with a pretend curiosity.

"The night before you killed Mary. I had a conversation with her. I kinda think you might benefit from the information I gathered. You know, in the slight possibility some guilt has reached you after she bled out."

I explain and he doesn't talk, but the look in his eyes, is telling me everything I need to know. My man has been tormenting himself after her death, mainly because I think deep down both of the twins wanted to believe the sob story Mary told them.

"She knew your parents died."

I tell him. His eyes grow wide.

"You must be kidding!"

"That is not all; she never wanted you. The only reason she went to her sister was the fact that she knew she would turn her to their parents. She was so young that it would cause a scandal. Her parents would have done everything in their power to prevent that, and she was counting on it."

His eyes wandered out of the window in the empty parking lot. He is not going to say anything else; this is his way of letting me know. The conversation has ended.

The rain is getting heavy, and the sound of it washes all the pain and suffering. It is almost cathartic in a way. We sit in silence, watching the diner.

It is mostly empty. Liam is sitting at his regular booth, and from time to time, Jess will go sit with him for a few minutes before she goes back to her regular duties. *They are getting comfortable.*

Mike

I am usually not the sensitive type. I don't believe sob stories, but something in me wanted to believe hers. I wanted to believe that she wouldn't toss us away like that.

She chose to look the other way while her brother and sister took the burden. They never wanted to have to deal with us; that, in a way, explains how easy it was for them to hurt us.

We belonged to the sister they never liked, a clear reminder of the disappointment of the family. We were the mistake, the burden. It is safe to assume she waited too long to tell them, trying to come up with a plan, most likely. Because I don't see a reason for them not forcing her to terminate the pregnancy instead.

I remember all the Sunday mornings our grandmother forced us to sit in church. She died when we were five, but until that point, church was a weekly event. Then her children made sure to teach us about the importance of God and religion. You know, in the meantime, of getting abused, starved, and neglected.

Now I don't think any of us believes in God. I don't think he would approve of our lifestyle choices. I would like to believe something greater than us exists, but I am not sure if I believe all the teachings of the church.

I am pretty sure I have seen Liam pray once. It was a few months after the fire; he was still struggling to shed our previous way of living. Still terrified every time an authority figure raised their voice at him.

Months passed before he could let Nate's father get close to him. He avoided the man with every ounce of his power. I think most people would have expected this behavior from me if they knew what was going on in my house, but my brother was always the sensitive one. I went through his horror alongside mine. I think the reason I became more cruel than him, is that I suffered more.

I had to survive more darkness. I had to endure more pain. Because of that, I became distant with my emotions and colder. My brother still has a heart, and I will go through everything and anything for him if that means he can keep it.

Liam's best quality is his empathy, his ability to care and be there for you, no matter what you do. His forgiving nature was always his biggest flaw, but at the same time, his best quality.

In another lifetime, I think Jess would be good for him. I see him, how he smiles while watching her work, and part of me wishes he could stay behind. Pick up a normal job, live his days having babies with her. I am sure it has crossed his mind once or twice already. He will never leave us, but I wish he would. He deserves to be happy, and he is not with us.

Liam

I have a bad feeling about this. Something is off. Those two have been whispering and planning something. I am driving tonight. Nate never lets me drive. He is also never in the back with the prey; something is going very wrong.

We are waiting next to a church. Mike claimed it would be more fun to pick her up after an AA meeting. My mask is sitting on my lap, and my eyes travel out of the car's window, thinking of the woman I have been falling in love with.

The van's back doors open, and both men jump out and a scream echoes through the night. I look into the rare view mirror as they drag a brunette wearing a pink dress, kicking and screaming into the car. She is pleading for mercy for help but her pleas reach no one and I start driving.

A short drive after - everything is too close in this town - we arrive at the maze. We get out of the car quickly, *somethings is wrong.*

Mike and I, both hop out at the same time and onto our bikes. Nate is holding a rope attached to a woman's tied hands.

"Are you ready to see our new little prey?"

Mike asks with a sinister laugh, that causes me chills.

"You will love this one."

Nate follows before he removes the hood from the woman's head.

Her eyes grow wide as she recognizes me, and I freeze in my seat not knowing what to do next.

Mike revs his bike and greets her.

"Hello angel."

She looks at me then back at the boys. Nate's voice comes next.

"If you reach the scarecrow, we will let you go, but keep in mind no one ever did. We have been playing this game for a long time."

The familiar instructions sound like a dream.

"Three rules: You get five minutes head start. You are allowed to only run through the maze If dawn comes first, before we find you or you reach the scarecrow, you may try again tomorrow."

Mike's voice sounds more evil than usual.

Nate takes a turn, his voice low almost like a growl.

"Run darling."

We know the maze to a point, that we could be hunting her blindfolded, and she would still not escape. It is the first thing we learn in a new town, our hunting grounds. Never a woman has managed to escape us. Jessica will be no different unless I help her. But the two men know that already and counting on it, I am sure.

This will end badly either way. There is nothing I can do, to save her and as the minutes pass, and I see her run, I realize the game has begun.

"You really thought we wouldn't find out?" Nate asks me.

"I just needed something to myself." I say defeated.

"Now you will have to share. Is she as good as Nate described her moans?"

THEIR DEADLY GAME

The words coming out of Mike register, and before I can say anything he revs his bike, and takes off. The game is different tonight.

Jessica

The man gives me the instructions to a twisted game they seem to want to play, my eyes are locked on Liam the entire time. He looks as terrified as I do. I am not sure if this was the plan all along or if he is trapped in this like myself.

"Run darling."

The dark-haired man tells me, and I hear the blonde's laugh, as I obey and start running. Panic sets in, as I dash through the darkening maze, Liam's terrified gaze still fixed on me.

I dare not to look back, fearing what I might see, and instead focus on putting as much distance between us as possible. The sound of their motorcycles behind me grows fainter, and I wonder if Liam is hunting me like they are, or if he is on my side.

Okay, Jessica, you need a plan. I think to myself as I try to remember the maze. We used to come here as kids every Halloween, during the celebrations. There is a scarecrow in the middle. I know how to get there. I used to play this game a lot with my friends. We would split and see who got there first. There are four ways to get there. I am on the path Alan used to always pick. It is the longest path.

I just need to switch between paths until they lose me. Then pick the shortest and get to the scarecrow. If that fails, I just need to hide until dawn, which should be in a few hours. *You got this Jessica.* I hype myself up.

I hear someone approach, and I hide in the closest dark corner, the lack of light sealing me from his eyes. I notice his blonde hair and the tattoos on his neck. *Definitely avoid that one.* I make a mental note.

Another motorcycle approaches from the back, and I hear Liam's familiar voice.

"She went that way."

He tells the blonde and points in the opposite direction of where I am.

"Let's go!"

The other guy screams and takes off.

"Right behind you."

Liam gets off his bike instead. He is walking slowly toward me, closing the distance between us. I am ready to scream, when his hand covers my mouth.

"I promise. I knew nothing about this." He whispers.

"This is not our first game, and you probably have figured it out by now."

He takes his hand away, and I turn around to face him.

"Yes, I figured." I respond.

"I am sorry I got you into this, but I am not sure I can get you out." His voice is sincere and full of pain.

"I have a plan."

I tell him, and his eyes lock with mine.

"I know the maze; I was playing here as a kid every Halloween, my friends and I used to pick a path and see who would get to the scarecrow first. I got this. I will get to it tonight or the next night.

Whichever it is, I got this."

I assure him and he gives me a forced smile.

"Liam!"

Someone calls, and the man in front of me gestures silently to be quiet.

"I am here."

He responds and gets back on his motorcycle, taking off towards the spot the man's voice was coming from.

I start running again, looking back to see if anyone follows me when I crash on something hard. I turn around to look and my eyes travel up to a face with a sinister smile.

"Hello Darling."

His voice sounds sadistic. I can't help how wet this chase has gotten me, his voice making it worse. *Not now, traitor.* I remind myself, as his hand wraps around my neck and he licks my lips.

"You do taste nice."

His voice is a whisper and then gets louder announcing.

"I got her."

It's not long before Liam and the blonde dude arrive.

"Little Jessica got caught."

The blonde teases, as he approaches from behind and leans to the man who holds me by my neck, claiming his lips. *Fuck this is hot. No! Jessica, focus! It is not the time to get horny.*

"What do you say, Liam, ready to share your toy?"

The one holding me says, and the blonde one cuts my dress letting it fall to the ground. A gasp escapes me and I clench my thighs to hide the moisture between my legs.

Liam's eyes grow wide, and he takes a step back, observing them.

"This isn't what I signed up for."

He mutters to himself.

The man holding me tugs at my hair, pulling my head back, forcing me to look at the smirking blonde.

"You're ours now."

He tells me, his tone is menacing.

My heart races, and I try to fight the heat that I can feel rising between my thighs. I swallow hard, trying to ignore my body's reaction.

"Let's have some fun."

The blonde dude chuckles, as he unzips his pants. I can feel the cold steel of the blade at my throat, pressing against my skin.

A strange feeling but arousing at the same time. Liam approaches and pulls me on him, taking my lower lip between his teeth, a soft bite, that makes me even more wet.

I used to always have those fantasies of multiple men, with masks, fucking me somewhere remotely, where my screams can't be heard. I used those to get off in the middle of the night, gasping for air trying to hide my moans behind my locked bedroom door. And now that I am here with these three men, I realize those fantasies were nothing against reality.

Liam's hands travel on my body and he whispers in my ear .

"This is Nate."

He points to the dark-haired guy, that had a grip on my neck a moment earlier.

"And this is my brother Mike."

He points to the dickish blonde guy.

Then he continues, in a voice I am only able to hear.

"If you want to run just say so, I will help you escape, but I can see how your body reacts already and I think you are into this as much as I am. I don't mind sharing."

He tells me and I give him the okay look, no need to say more. He throws my body on Nate before I can react.

"Let's play."

He tells him and Nate cuts the rope around my hands, that was still keeping them tied together.

Mike approaches and falls on his knees, pulling my right leg on his shoulder. He cuts my underwear with his knife, and tosses the ruined fabric to the side. His tongue flicks on my clit, and I can't help but lean back on Nate.

Nate bites my neck, and trails kisses as he pinches my nipples over the fabric of my bra. Liam comes closer and uses his knife to cut the remaining clothing off my body. He leans in and kisses me and I return his kiss moaning against his lips, while his brother eats my pussy.

Nate drops himself to the ground, taking my body with him. He lays me on the hay, Mike re-adjusts himself and drops down between my legs again. He keeps licking me, fucking me with his tongue, my body is shaking at his touch.

"Please I need more."

I beg them, but I am not sure what I am begging for.

Nate unbuttons his jeans and takes his cock out stroking himself before he turns to me, he sits next to me and tells me.

"Sit on my cock darling."

I look up to Liam who repeats the order.

"Make yourself come on his cock sweetheart."

I nod and slowly get on top of him.

I see Mike as he sets his own dick free and lines up behind me.

"Be a good girl and make them happy."

Liam tells me

I take Nate's cock in my hand and help it slowly inside me. He is big and takes me a minute before I can move.

"Fuck, you feel so good darling." He tells me as he moves slowly under me.

He is fucking me painfully slow, and I moan against his lips as he bites the bottom one sending pain through my body.

Mike grabs my ass and he pushes inside me from behind, hard and fast and I moan louder not being able to keep myself. Liam is now stroking himself and he comes closer, with a fist full of my hair he turns my head towards him.

"Open."

He tells me and I do as I am told.

He pushes inside my mouth again and again, his voice sounds like from another reality.

"Good girl, look at you being fucked in every hole."

He fucks my mouth harder, I struggle to breathe as my orgasm reaches me like a wave.

"Good girl come for us."

Nate praises from underneath me, and Mike fucks my ass harder chasing his own orgasm. I feel him spilling inside me moments later, and Nate follows him.

"Fuck, such a good girl darling. You doing so good."

Nate praises and I feel Liam's cock twitch in my mouth, hot strings of cum shoot down my throat and I savor every drop.

"Good girl."

He tells me and wipes a drop of his release from my lips. My eyes close shut, the tension of the moment getting to me finally.

"Boys, let's get her home!"

Nate calls and Mike is helping me up.

I feel Nate's arm wrap around me and I am being carried back to the van.

"You did so well sweetheart." Liam tells me and kisses my temple.

When we reach the car, He doesn't put me in the back this time. Liam climbs in the passenger's seat and opens his arms. His friend places me on his lap. He hugs my body, trailing circles on my back with his fingertips, as the rest of the guys get in the car and we drive *home*.

Liam

Nate is driving us home, I am in the passenger seat with a sleeping Jessica on my lap and a smirking Mike squeezed between myself and the driver's seat. He is looking at me with that look I know all too well, the one that decorates his face as a huge *fuck you* full of misfit.

"So, how pissed are you Liam?"

I chuckle, my gaze turns back to Jessica. *She did so well, my pretty girl.*

"I would have shared, if you asked me nicely."

I say and both men laugh.

"You know this is not how I planned to punish you, but I am not pissed about it."

Nate informs me and I laugh.

As we arrive at the house Nate gets out of the car first, he circles it and comes to my door. I open it, and he lifts Jessica off my arms.

"Are you sure you don't want us to take her to her house?"

Mike questions, his voice low to not wake her up.

I nod, she is not happy there and I am not ready to let her go, now that the guys know about her I have no reason to let her go as for now.

"Take her to my room."

My bed is bigger, I can tell the guys are not planning to leave her either. I follow Nate and Mike as they carry our sleeping girl to my room.

Nate stands on the side of the bathroom's door, waiting for us to get the shower ready for Jessica. She is dirty and full of cum, a much-needed shower, this will be.

Mike takes a pair of boxers and a t-shirt that seems too big for Jessica, but luckily will cover enough for her to feel comfortable here. I step into the bathroom and turn on the water in the shower, I shed my clothes and move closer to Nate and Jessica.

Shaking slightly Jessica's sleeping body I say, my voice barely above a whisper.

"Time to wake up sweetheart, we need to clean you up."

Her eyes open, she mumbles a positive response, as I take her off Nate's arms. I carry her to the shower and I step inside. I pull her under the water, the warm liquid hitting our skin with a soothing effect. A sweet little moan escapes her and I understand she must be feeling sore, I help her stand and Mike gets in the shower with us. I will admit this is more than I want to see of my brother but at this point this twisted situation makes sense.

He pours some shampoo on her hair and washes it, while I use the shower gel to wash her body. She leans against his body as we clean her. When we are done, Nate is waiting outside with a towel to wrap around her.

He helps her into the room, and into my clothes. She looks amazing even in a man's t-shirt and boxers. I can't keep myself from feeling this sense of sudden happiness that this moment has to offer. I look around to my family taking care of her and in this moment I have everything I would ever wish for.

I am not the type of man to get attached to a woman. I have gone through so much loss in my life that getting attached is never the goal. But this woman, has something else. Something different and unique, that I could never really pinpoint my mind on, more likely a sense than a specific quality. What makes her unique, is the feelings she ignites inside me.

She gets under the covers, and I follow her pulling the covers on her body and mine. I open my arms and she crawls right in. I look around the room, observing the two men that exchange a series of looks. They both move to the bed. Mike gets next to Jessica and Nate is right behind him. He wraps him into a tight cuddle and Mike kisses his lips, as a form of *goodnight*.

We fall asleep and it is as peaceful as I would have imagined, the first night that any of us actually got some decent sleep since we got in this town. Maybe the first night after years of sleepless nights of blood, and horror.

Jessica

I am waking up slowly as Liam kisses the side of my neck and shoulder. His hand travels between my legs and I feel his hard cock pressing on my ass. I stir and turn my head to look at him. He gives me an innocent smile and circles my clit with his fingers.

"Good morning."

I mumble between moans and sleepiness.

He chuckles.

"Good morning sweetheart."

He pushes a finger inside me, and my head tilts, finding a place between his shoulder and neck.

"Sweetheart don't wake them up."

He warns, and I now notice the two guys sleeping next to us.

Before I can process what Is happening he is pushing inside my ass.

"I wanted to fuck your ass since I met you."

He tells me as he slowly moves in and out of me, with his fingers fucking my pussy.

I bite my lips trying not to moan, already on the urge of my orgasm. It is like he knows my body too well because he speeds up fucking me harder and his nails dig on my thigh as a warning to keep silent.

"Come for me sweetheart."

He orders and I am already so close, I don't need him to tell me twice, my pussy starts pulsing around his fingers the moment his words leave him.

"Good girl."

He praises and fucks me harder causing me a mix of pain and pleasure, as he is spilling inside me finding his own orgasm.

I am trying to catch my breath, he slips out of me and gets off the bed. He pulls my hand and helps me stand.

"Let's shower and get some breakfast."

He announces in a whisper, and I chuckle as I look back at the two men still sleeping deeply.

I follow him to the shower and I pull the t-shirt, I am wearing over my head.

I am looking around for the boxers, and I realize he must have removed them from me in my sleep.

I step into the shower, closing the space between us, and he leans down to place a soft kiss on my lips. I smile at his touch; he is being so sweet, making my heart swell.

We finish our shower and move to the kitchen, making breakfast while the guys wake up before they join us. The rest of the morning follows the same pattern of passion and affection, making me wonder how long this will last.

Liam

It has been a few hours since this morning, and we all have found ourselves gathered in front of the fireplace in Mike's room. Sitting on some pillows he has set on the floor as a little reading corner for himself, Jessica curled up on my side while my brother is in the arms of his boyfriend. We all seem too content for this to be real.

"Tell me about the hunts."

Jessica breaks the silence with her demand, causing a stir among the three of us.

No one talks until Nate speaks up, always the one to lead the group when none of us has anything to say.

"They started after college. We hunt 2-5 women in each town and move on. They never end like this."

He tells her. I can tell he was hoping to scare her enough to not ask more, but I see our girl's fire ignite and she asks again.

"How many women have you killed in this town ?"

She presses.

"Five, we need to move soon. They are starting to suspect the missing women reports."

He informs her. *I know it is a lie, no women have been reported missing so far.*

"They don't have any clues as it is for now though".

He is trying to scare her, but I can see the wheels turning inside her head.

"So where are we going next?"

She asks, pressing with a hint of authority, demanding to be included.

Nate chuckles.

"Oh, are you joining us darling?"

He asks her with a teasing tone, and none of us expect her to say this but she does.

"Yes, I am. You chased me through a fucking maze and gave me the best orgasms I ever had. Of course I am coming with you, did you expect to be done with me that easy?"

Laughs fill the room and I kiss her temple, she smiles back at me.

"Good girl, I would never leave you anyway."

She nods acknowledging my words, the other men seem to be oblivious about our little secret.

What Jessica seems to be oblivious to is that she is stuck with us too. None of us plan to leave her behind, and we don't need to communicate this to know we all think the same.

Jessica

"**S**o where are we going next?"

I repeat my question. All three of my men stay quiet for a second too long.

Mike smiles in a meaningful way to his brother and I feel Liam as he nods back to him in agreement.

"New York." Mike announces "Time for a break from the game boys."

But before I can say anything, Nate speaks up.

"It is about time. I am getting too old to be digging graves man."

Liam frowns at his words.

"Like any of you have dug any of them."

He responds.

Laughter fills the room once more. I realize at this moment how fucked up the situation is, but I can't keep myself from getting wet at the idea of these three dangerous men, only melting for me.

I take Liam's hand, guiding between my legs and he gets the message right away as he slips it inside the pair of boxers, I am wearing finding my clit. His fingertips work my clit, while his mouth nibbles and trails kisses on the side of my neck and shoulder.

Mike gets on his knees jend crawls to us closing the space, while Nate takes out his cock, stands and walks pumping his length in his hand. He grabs me by my hair, bringing me right where he wants me, guiding my lips around his cock and I take him inside my mouth, tearing up on the size of him reaching the back of my throat, while he fucks my face.

Liam lifts me to sit on his cock as he lays back on the pillows and Mike now is pressing his cock against my entrance while his brother is inside my ass. They both fuck me hard and I moan around Nate's dick feeling him, getting closer before he spills down my throat.

I swallow every drop, and he praises me.

" Good girl darling."

Mike pumps inside me faster and I feel the wave of my orgasm as both men spill inside me. We all fall back on the pillows, catching our breaths.

"Well, a few more nights with Jess, and I might forget the hunts all together." Mike announces to the room.

Everyone laughs at the prospect of this crazy man ever being domesticated and content only with this.

Mike

I am sitting with Jessica on the couch, her legs draped over mine and my laptop set on hers. We have been scrolling through the pages of her former classmates, people who made her life miserable when she was just a kid herself, trying to navigate life without a mother.

My heart would ache for her if I had one, but still, sadness fills me at the thought of Jessica being so lost and hurt. Those people made an already hard situation worse, and I can't keep myself from getting angry.

"This is Lindsay."

She tells me, keeping her voice at a whisper level.

I check the photo she just showed me; the woman has red hair and is smiling, but her smile is not genuine. She is putting on a persona for her social media; this is clear enough for me to notice.

"Tell me about her, angel."

I say, checking to see if the guys have noticed us yet.

Liam is still working on whatever Nate has assigned him. We are safe for now.

"She was the popular girl in my high school."

She begins to tell me.

"She used to make jokes during class, but never anything harmful, up to the point when I stopped attending school. She once visited the diner and ordered every milkshake on the menu. She didn't touch any of it, and when it was time to pay she got up and poured the first two on my head. She walked away without saying anything, and I saw from the window that a bunch of guys from the football team were outside recording what happened."

I am trying not to get mad at what she said, but now I get why she is showing me those people; she wants to hunt.

"Angel, why are you showing me this?"

Her eyes avoid mine when she tells me.

"I want to hunt her in the maze like you did me."

The fuck! She is not serious, right? She can't be.

"You are joking, right?"

I question, and she shakes her head.

"I want to teach her a lesson."

"You know the women in our game usually don't get out alive, right?"

I try to explain to her the importance of her request, but I am clearly not doing a good job. "She deserves it!"

Jessica tells me.

Liam

It's been a few days already with Jessica in the house. We are getting ready to move back to New York. Nate is arranging everything on the phone for our apartment to be ready while Mike and Jessica are being sneaky about something on Mike's laptop. I am surprised this thing even works with the screen shattered.

"What are you doing?"

I ask as I sneak on them from behind. Mike closes the screen in a hurry.

And Jessica pretends to inspect her nails. I circle the couch and stand in front of her, pushing her chin up to look at me with my hand.

"Sweetheart, I asked you a question." I press.

A sinister smile forms on her lips a matching one of my brother's who now is turning the laptop screen my way to see what they were looking at.

"Her name is Lindsay." Jessica states. "We thought we should do a last hunt before leaving here. I want to join."

Her voice is bubbly and excited.

"You are joking, right?"

I ask in disbelief.

"Nate get the fuck in here, these two are planning to kidnap a woman!"

I yell, like we haven't done worse things, but Jessica is not like that. *We are a really bad influence on this girl, aren't we?*

Nate bursts into the living room with a confused look on his face.

"Say what now?"

I am showing him Mike's laptop, letting the photos of the fiery redhead and these two idiots planning to kidnap do the talking instead.

"I thought we all agreed on a break."

Nate is rubbing his temples like he is getting a headache. I don't know if I should laugh or not, but this situation is so messed up that it is almost hilarious.

"Fine."

Nate agrees finally, and now I am sure I am the only sane person in this group of heathens I am surrounding myself with.

"One last hunt. Come on, darling, let's find you a motorcycle to ride." Nate declares.

Nate

I am driving the familiar way to the maze, with Liam in the passenger seat and a redhead tied up in the back. Mike and Jessica are already there, waiting for us.

"This is a really bad idea." Liam states.

I couldn't agree more. None of us expected Jessica to turn out this way. She is the female version of Mike, that somehow can get all three of us hard at the same time, and make us follow her like lost puppies.

I glance at Liam, his brow furrowed in concern as he stares out the window at the passing trees. The redhead in the back stirs, mumbling something through the gag. I grip the steering wheel tighter, feeling the weight of our situation pressing down on me.

This will not end well for any of us. Jessica was not supposed to turn out this way. She wasn't supposed to be okay with what we are, let alone join the games.

She is doing that willingly, she chose the victim. She even proposed the hunt. Mike told me as much, when I questioned him after they announced to us, that we were hunting tonight. He is surprisingly fine with it, and I am not sure, if there is something we don't know about this woman that Jess shared with him.

Maybe he saw something familiar in Jess, maybe she has a need for it like he does, and will make no sense to me or Liam.

It is also a possibility he went completely crazy, and now brings more people into this madness by boredom.

I drive right to the entrance of the maze and park next to the two bikes already parked there. Mine and Liam's are in the back with the redhead. I turn to look at him in the passenger seat, and he shakes his head as he gets out of the car.

We approach Mike and Jessica; I can see the excitement in her eyes. She is dressed in black. A leather jacket, similar to what the twins have always worn, completes her outfit.

They left the house before us, and now I know why.

"Did some shopping, I see."

I point out, and Jessica twirls to show me her outfit.

Liam's glare now can cut glass, and I can feel his furious gaze on my back, as he opens the back door of the van taking out the redhead.

Jessica approaches with a knife and cuts the redhead's binds. She strokes her face with her fingertips and removes a red curly piece of hair in front of her eyes, tucking it behind the redhead's ear.

"Rules are simple."

Jessica's voice sounds cold and distant.

"There is a scarecrow in the middle of the maze. Get there and you are safe. If any of us catches you though, you are fair game. If you manage to hide until dawn you can try again tomorrow."

She recites the rules like I did the first night we brought her here. I see the boys moving on their bikes already. I take mine as well and Jessica now pulls the redhead from her hair to the edge of the maze.

"Be a good girl and start running."

She taunts.

The redhead's eyes grow wide with fear and she starts running. Her movements are slow and we allow her a head start, even though she is doing a terrible job of running for her life.

The woman is terrified and even the slightest sound makes her jump. I pity her in a way. The game has become complicated, since Jessica joined us. I am pretty sure Liam agrees with me, as he deliberately lets the woman slip out when he gets closer to her. I give him a well-known look, that she won't escape here alive either way, but I understand why he tried to give her a better chance of survival.

The woman turns left and right, and we are stalking close by as she reaches the scarecrow. She is one of the locals, close to Jessica's age, and I am assuming from her reaction that they know each other. Jessica told us she used to play in the maze as a teenager on Halloween. It is safe to assume this woman played the same games.

Jessica appears from behind her, and I follow her, the sound making the woman turn to face us. The twins are now approaching her from the other way.

"I reached the scarecrow."

She announces, and Jessica laughs.

"I am safe; I reached the scarecrow." She repeats.

They always believe the stupid rules, and every time they think, they have found some ally among us.

Mike laughs at her statement, and Liam grabs her by her throat pulling her against his body. He is whispering in her ear something, I can't hear from where I stand.

Mike takes his blade and slices her cheek, blood floods from the wound and the woman gasps, her tears now mixing with her blood. He licks the blood and winks at her.

"You were never safe doll."

Liam tells her and slices her throat, the moment he finishes his sentence.

Jessica releases a happy scream, too excited from the hunt and we all get on our motorcycles to return back to where we left the van. I place the dead woman on mine to carry back.

When we reach the entrance of the maze, where the van is parked, I place her body in the back inside the plastic body bag, we keep back there.

I toss the keys to Liam who is usually in charge of disposing the bodies, but he shakes his head.

Mike gets the keys from him, before he can say anything, and I know that Liam right now is spiraling but trying his best to hide it from Jessica.

"Come on darling let's go home to get you cleaned up."

I say inspecting Jessica who somehow got blood on her, she must have been close when Liam sliced the woman's throat. She smiles and gets on her bike as we all drive back to the house.

Mike

I have been the one doing the kills half the time. Sometimes it is Nate who pulls the trigger or slices a throat, but tonight was the first time Liam put his blade in one of the women.

Deep down we all knew at this point he wanted to save Jessica from doing it. *Except of Jessica, of course.*

She surprised everyone with how willing was to participate, in fact, tonight's hunt was all her. I barely wanted to participate myself but after I saw her eyes while she was showing me the photos of this woman. I knew she needed this as much as I need the hunts.

She was getting revenge, and that I can understand. This woman is hell herself. She is fire. The one we should fear, not the other way around.

I drive the three hours distance to the location, we have been dumping the bodies since we moved here. This is always our way of operating.

We choose a town to move in and hunt, and another as a dumping ground. We move monthly. By the time the authorities figure it out, we have moved on to a different location, and due to the fact that we have been doing this for years, I would say they have no clue the disappearances are connected.

No bodies except the first have been discovered, Nate did a terrible job hiding it. He has some great qualities, but attention to detail was never one of them.

Liam came up with that plan years ago after Nate's failure, and he is so good at planning that I would bet my left kidney. They have no clue that the missing women are connected.

The fact that they are not talking with each other or calling in the big guns to help them is to our advantage.

They have absolutely no chance of figuring it out. Small-town police departments are always not equipped to handle our type of evil.

In the eyes of the law, we are three men, well-educated, extremely rich, with manners and authority, traveling the world after the dead of our parents.

Since we moved into Nate's house when we were kids and were officially adopted before becoming adults, my brother and I are considered, in the eyes of the law, their kids as much as Nate. Ironic, isn't it? How well we have bonded over the years would turn heads.

I arrive at the remote land where we have chosen to bury the women, we have murdered on this side of the country, and I park a good distance from the spot. I slide the van's side door open, and take out my shovel and the redhead's lifeless body.

Tonight, things have changed in a lot of ways.

Not only did we have a woman participating in a different way in the chase, but my brother drew blood and took a life. I am sure he is tormenting himself over it. Luckily he has Jess to keep him busy. While I hide the evidence of our latest crime.

I drag the woman's lifeless body to the spot, where Liam has buried the rest of them and begin to dig. Light rain starts to fall, not enough to ruin my plans but as needed to cover my tracks after I am done. A detail I have learned from Liam, he is always saying how rain can work in his favor and now I am hoping he is right.

This town has been the perfect dump site. Not much activity at night, and the weather is often filled with rain and mist. When the hole in the ground is deep enough I drag her body pushing it inside

I begin to shovel dirt over the woman's body. Each scoop of dirt feels like a burden, a symbol of the responsibility we carry with us. As the grave is nearly filled, I take one last look. This woman is no longer the person she once was, she has become a symbol of our twisted game.

I am usually not the guilty type. But tonight I don't believe any of us, other than Jessica, truly wanted to participate.

It should be a red flag, that this woman, not only is fine with dating three serial killers, but also wants in on the action.

I am a lot of things, reasonable is not one of them. A twisted part of me gets hard on the thought of her enjoying the kills as much as I do. Another is worried what will happen, if we piss her off.

It must be around five in the morning when I arrive at the house. I enter through the front door and notice Jessica is sitting on the window ledge where my brother usually sits.

This girl has a piece of every single one of us if you notice her long enough: The calculating nature of Nate, my impulsive, unhinged need for a hunt, and Liam's tendency to shut down when things get too much. She is our equal in every way, and if we are not careful, she will be the end of us.

I have been noticing her since she entered our lives. She always seems to be happy and bubbly. The guys love that about her, I am sure, but there are moments like this one. When she gets dark and gloomy. A look in her eyes that looks almost as dark as night.

She is quick to shed it when someone notices, a strong girl in every way, and I can't help myself from wondering what happened to her. I am pretty sure we are not the reason for her sorrow, or at least I hope we are not.

This woman has an amazing, strong personality, a captivating nature in every sense. It is no surprise to me that all three of us are head over heels for her. In fact, I wish she had entered our lives earlier; maybe some of the things we have been through would look less horrible with her in them.

I step closer to her, but she doesn't seem to notice I have entered the house at all, and I observe how small and vulnerable she looks at this moment.

"What troubles you, angel?"

I ask her, keeping my voice low.

She turns her head to look at me and I notice the tears in her eyes. Something inside me, breaks at the sight of her crying.

"Who hurt you?"

I press.

"Tell me what happened?"

And then her body language changes.

"I just wonder."

She starts, taking a pause, gathering herself.

"What would be different if my mother were still here."

Her words confuse me, and I wonder what happened before I can stop myself from asking the words, leaving my lips.

"What happened to your mother?"

She turns her head away from me, her eyes fixating on a tree in the backyard.

"She died when I was ten."

She tells me, and I take the seat next to her, waiting for her to share the parts of her story she is willing to, without pressing more.

I would love to press her right now, but I need her to share this willingly. I have always had the need to take the pain away from the people I love. Liam's tears and the belt marks on his skin, hunted me more than my own. Nate's sobs in his sleep turned my dreams into nightmares when the horrors in my life couldn't. I would end everyone and everything for those two and now Jessica seems to have joined that list. *I would turn the world upside down, if it meant she won't shed another tear but I don't tell her that. She doesn't need to know.*

Jessica

Mike is sitting next to me, his hand barely touching mine as we sit on the window ledge looking outside, as the first light of dawn bursts through the tree line of the property. I can tell he wants to ask more, know more, but he doesn't, and as much as I appreciate it, I want to share this with him.

I continue telling him what I have not shared with anyone before.

"I remember the days leading to the birth of my baby brother. My mother was so happy."

My words barely come out. From the way Mike is looking at me right now, I can tell the subject might be a little too close to home for him as well.

He doesn't say anything. He is letting me speak, sharing my pain, like it is the most important thing for him in this world.

"When her water broke, we called the midwife to the house; my mother was screaming for dear God on her bedroom floor. My father was pacing in the hallway, and I knew something was very wrong."

My voice barely comes out but I need to share this with him.

I need him to know my demons if I want him to share his.

"She was a brave woman, who fought until her last breath. She pushed with every ounce of her strength. She was screaming, scratching the floor, in pure agony. And as the first cry of my brother was heard, my mother took her last breath, and the world became a dark place."

"Jessica I am so sorry, you don't need to tell me the rest if it pains you."

He tells me and wipes a tear off my cheek.

"No."

I respond firmly.

"I want to."

I take a sharp breath before continuing, it pains me to remember but needs to be done.

"Forty eight hours hours he lived, my brother, that is, I never knew what was wrong with him. My father just arranged for both their funerals. He refused to get an autopsy. He did not want to know the reason, and in a way, I don't blame him. I did everything in my power to help that baby. He kept crying for all those hours he was alive. His cries haunt me to this day."

I hide my face between my hands. Now sobbing silently, embarrassed to look at his face.

Mike pulls me closer and holds me tight, stroking my hair and whispering to me.

"Everything will be fine Jess."

I would give anything to believe him. Anything to feel actually safe, not just for a few moments.

I know I need to continue, I need to tell him everything. I might not have another chance to share my story with someone. I am not a fool to think the guys will stay with me, after realizing how broken I am. Deep down I hope if I share this side of me, they will realize I belong with them. *I am as broken as all of them. I belong with them.*

"After their funerals, my father lost himself in his bottle. I was left alone to fend for myself. He did not care about me in the slightest. He kept food on the table and maintained the house with whatever job he could find for a short period of time until they realized his alcohol problem and fired him. The debt kept growing, so when I turned sixteen, I decided to quit school and start working."

I tell him between sobs and tears.

"I blamed myself for what happened. Maybe if I had noticed earlier that something was wrong. Maybe if I had begged him to take her to the hospital. They might have lived. I tried everything in my power to help him after, but it feels like my father died alongside my mother all those years ago."

A sigh of relief escapes me, finally sharing this part of myself feels like an elephant has moved his foot from my heart. Mike stays silent. He continues holding me. I sob in his arms, feeling safe and loved. Deep down, I am sure this won't last, but right now I savor every bit of affection he has to offer.

Liam

It is a little after nine when Mike and Jessica burst into my bedroom, where myself and Nate have been sleeping after our night with Jess. Each of them holding one mug for themselves and one for each of us, they set the mugs on the dresser before joining us in bed. Mike settles in the arms of a very sleepy Nate and pulls Jessica against his as I settle on her side, claiming her lips with mine.

"Good morning beautiful."

I greet her and I see Mike making a face and sticking his tongue out as a greeting. I give him a vulgar gesture in return and both of them laugh.

"Why are you all in my bed?"

Nate asks, and laughs are bursting through the room again.

"Not to break your bubble buddy, but you are in my bed."

Nate growls, his eyes searching for something.

"I smell coffee." He murmurs.

Jessica gets off the bed, returning with his mug. He takes the mug she is offering, and Jessica bows with grace.

"At your service, sir."

She laughs again. Her laugh is the most amazing sound I have heard in my entire life.

This is how I want to spend every morning from now on. With my family all in one place, laughter, jokes, and good coffee. I take the mug Jessica now is offering me, and I bring it to my lips. A long sip of the hot liquid after I change my mind; this *is not good coffee.*

"We should go to Rosa's for coffee."

I announce, and I see Jessica's eyes grow distant.

"I have told them I am sick for a few days now, but I am assuming I should give Rosa my notice since we are moving to New York, right?"

She questions, Nate nods in agreement but we are all questioning this decision in silence.

Even though a selfish part of me wants to keep Jessica forever, her behavior last night was concerning to all of us. Not only she joined the hunt but was also the one to plan it. This girl who was once the polite waitress in my favorite diner. The one to greet everyone with a smile and care for them, this girl now is eager to dip her hands in blood.

If we care as much as we claim we do, we should leave her to her peaceful way of living, her drunk father to take care of and her diner shifts to keep her busy. Instead of bringing her with us to a life of horror and blood.

"Three men and their girlfriend go to dinner."

Mike jokes, and Jessica laughs from behind me. She is walking next to Nate, and his arm is draped over her shoulder as we pass through the front entrance of Rosa's Dinner.

Mike is walking beside me and we head to my regular booth, while Nate and Jess have stopped to talk to the cook, who is happy to see his best friend well and smiling.

After all, she did tell everyone that she was taking a few days off to recover from sickness while she was living under our roof, hunting a redheaded woman in a maze. *This is messed up, Jessica.*

Rosa, a smiley old lady with grayish-blonde hair, approaches them from the back of the counter. She hugs Jess and offers her hand for Nate to shake; of course, our well-mannered good boy does as he is expected.

The view of the fancy-dressed Nate, shaking the old lady's hand, is poetic in a way. He doesn't belong in this life, but he has chosen to live through it for us.

It was a time in our lives when we tried the opposite way. Fitting into his world instead, going to fancy schools and living like we deserved all the luxury, should have been easy enough to manage, but not for us.

Mike always looked uncomfortable at every restaurant Nate's parents took us to, and I, myself, had no interest in any of that. It was clear enough to Nate that we would never be happy in that lifestyle. But what made it set in stone was the night of that college party.

The screams of our first victim, her blood in our hands, and the way my brother laughed, as he dipped his blade in her flesh, had formed a bond between the three of us that nothing could break. He knew he had to adjust to protect us. We all did in a way. You can't live in luxury and keep being undetected while killing your way across the country.

As they join us to the remote booth I have been sitting, every morning for the past month, I can't keep myself from thinking. We should not keep dragging Jess into our madness.

We chose this life, but she still has the opportunity to leave. Her hands are still clean from blood. All three of us now have taken a life, but she did nothing more than participate in the running. The only witness of yesterday's events, is now dead.

I made sure to be the one to kill the redhead to protect Jessica from doing it. I wanted to give her the opportunity to be able to escape us. I wanted her to have the opportunity to leave us, but the more time passes it is clear to all of us, she is not planning to do that.

Our food arrives, Jessica, ordered for all of us wanting to treat us to something nice. Alan did his best and the food is as delicious as every other time.

Pancakes with different topics are in front of us and Mike is digging like a feral animal on his plate. Nate is giving him a fierce look, and Jessica is ignoring both of them while she is picking apart her own food.

I just sip my coffee observing the three people I have been spending every living hour with, for the past few days, and my thoughts drift back to the night before.

I had never killed anyone before that night. I had made sure. I was only participating in the hunts, helping dispose of the bodies and organizing the kidnappings. I felt no need to take a life, but the adrenaline of the chase was enough of a high for me to keep taking part in them.

Someone outside of our little group might think that I didn't want to participate at all, and it will be a fair assumption. I didn't want to. I love my brother and my friend, so I stuck with them.

Mike found a way to cope with the horrors his stepfather caused him through that twisted little game, and one could argue Nate has a twisted nature of his own. I stuck around because I love them. I wanted to make sure they would never get caught.

I disposed every body myself, did the research for every victim, and made sure we stayed free. Now I need to make sure that, we will continue to be free. *She has to go.*

I stalked every victim, gathered information, and planned their abduction in such detail that would take days before they were announced missing. Even longer to assume dead, resulting in being nearly impossible for a serial killer to be assumed, as the reason for their murder. *I refuse to be caught ,because I fell in love with a woman.*

I made sure to stalk the news of every town we visited for months after our time there. I checked the social media of parents and close relatives, friends or boyfriends, husbands or fiances of the women we killed.

Every step I took all these years, was calculated in a way to ensure we never get caught. To ensure my brother and my friend would never have to be brought accountable for their actions. That I would never have to answer for mine.

Everyone had their role so far. Mike started the hunts, Nate likes the chase and kills, and I am always in charge of the clean up. It works for us. Jessica's entry into our little group has caused this dynamic to fall apart.

In the past we would all agree, Mike should never be trusted with clean up, we would not kill more than five women in one area, and we would never fuck one during our hunts. Of course, I am to blame for her entering our lives. I must be the one to make sure she leaves them as well. I am falling for her and I know the guys are too, but no woman is worth losing them. *She needs to go.*

Jessica

After we had our breakfast at Rosa's, the boys drove back to the house, and I took Liam's motorcycle to my father's house. We will be leaving soon, and I know he was not the best father, but I need to get some essentials; why not try for a little closure as well?

As I reach my father's driveway, I park the bike under a tree, shielding it from any view from the house. I take my keys out of my back pocket, and slowly, I reach the front door. I unlock with hesitation, not sure what I am going to tell my father. I don't expect him to have noticed how long was the last time he saw me or the fact that I have been gone for a few days now.

"Dad? It's me, Jessica."

I shout as I enter the house, but as I had expected, he doesn't respond and I yell again.

" Dad, Are you here?"

To my surprise, this time I do hear footsteps in return and my father soon appears from the living room.

But it is not the broken man I left here the night before the AA meeting, that stands in front of me. This man looks like my father, but he is not. He is clearly sober, well-dressed, and clean. The last memory of my father looking that way must be a few days before my mother's death.

"Jessica? I have been worried about you."

I'm just standing frozen in place, hearing him talk, unable to wrap my head around what I'm seeing.

"You are sober."

I state, not expecting much of a response.

"Yes. When you didn't return for the last few nights, I started thinking something happened to you. The idea of losing you too, brought me back from the nightmare, I was living in since your mother died. I thought my best chance of finding you would be to be sober, when I go to the police station to declare you missing."

I nod in understanding and walk towards the living room.

He follows me and continues telling me what I missed while gone.

"I got sober the next day, and I haven't had a drink since. It is almost a week now. I was going to head to the station today to file a report of you missing, but you don't look like you are." He notices.

"I am not; I was with some friends."

I tell him, but he shakes his head.

"Alan said he saw two men drag you inside a van after the meeting."

I laugh, even though this is true.

"No, Dad, Alan must have seen wrong. I am clearly fine."

I assure him.

He seems like he believes me.

"However, I did find a job in New York. My friends offered me to join them there. We leave in a few days, and I just need some clothes." I add.

"I understand; I will help you pack."

He offers, and I need to give him some reassurance that he won't be left to fend for himself just because I decided to leave everything and move.

"Dad, I have some money saved."

I hand him the envelope with nearly five thousand in it. I have saved every day I worked, part of my paycheck. I had planned to use the money to find an escape out of this town, but that has been offered to me by the guys anyway. They don't seem to struggle for money, and Nate already told me they will cover my expenses. I don't need the money anymore.

"I can't accept this, Jessica. Thank you, but I will refuse any more help from you. You have done so much for me in the past few years. You deserve to do something for yourself."

With that, he hands me the envelope back and leaves the room, but he pauses right before and adds .

"I found a job; I will start tomorrow. I will be okay. Good luck, Jess."

Without another word, he leaves the room. *Good luck to you, too.*

I head to my room and open my closet. I find a backpack and a suitcase. Walking to my dresser, I empty the first two drawers of underwear and other essentials into the backpack.

I walk to my bathroom and drop every skincare product and makeup I own, not that there is much. I was never into makeup and did not have anyone to teach me. My mother died before she could, and I had no friends in school.

I take the suitcase and open it on my bed, packing the rest of my clothes neatly while I type a message on my phone to Mike:

I am ready. Come pick me up with Liam.

I decide to spend the rest of the time here to have one last bath. I take the change of clothes I have kept out of the suitcase in the bathroom with me. I turn the hot water on to fill the bathtub, and I light the two candles I have in my bathroom.

That has been my own little ritual before bed, my favorite time of the day since I was a kid. I have memories of my mother preparing the same bath for me. I still use the same salts and soaps that she used. I open the bottle, the scents fill me, taking a moment to remember her. Before I drop some in the bath.

This is the only way. I need to do this. There is nothing keeping me here. I remind myself, as I enter the bathtub; the hot water brings a cozy sensation to my skin. I feel relaxed after years of feeling on the edge all the time. I am letting myself enjoy this for the last time while waiting for the guys to come pick me up.

Mike

I see the message I just received from Jessica. Ignoring it, I set my phone on the side, turning to my brother.

"You think we should leave her here?"

I ask again, and he nods.

"I usually try to stay out of situations like this, and you know it, Mike." Nate begins to tell me. "This time I am with Liam. She is unpredictable, this woman is crazy you can tell. Not only she was not scared after chasing her into a fucking maze in the middle of the night. After throwing her in the back of our van, may I add. She also arranged for another woman to be chased the next day, and participated willingly."

He is not wrong, she is crazy, we can agree on that.

"I know her behavior is weird." I tell them.

Before Nate can say anything else Liam speaks.

"I have fallen for her as much as you have I am sure. After all, I have been stalking her since the day after our first hunt here. She is amazing, I wish we could keep her. But she is as much of a liability as if we had let Mary live."

Good one brother; compare the woman we all love to the bitch that birthed us, only to hand us to our worst nightmares.

I don't tell him that, though; instead, I say, "I agree. We should leave now because she is waiting. Who knows how she will react if we don't pick her up soon".

They agree and leave the room to pack, as I do the same.

I go to my room, take my suitcase from under the bed, I open it and start throwing the basic things we have brought here. We always travel light. We have two vans big enough for our things and our bikes.

The plan is always the same, we separate. Liam takes the black van we use to transport the bikes.

Nate takes the white one, we use to kidnap the women with our stuff in the back instead of some slut we picked up. I usually join Nate.

We change our license plates before the trip, and we change them again when we arrive in the new town. We also remove the ones from the bikes and dispose of them, with anything else that might link us to the previous town.

Takes only an hour for us to pack, before we meet downstairs. Liam is filling the white van with our suitcases and the dog. Nate is packing the bikes minus Liam's.

"Are we going to pick up your bike?" He asks him.

"No, we won't; she will notice if we do. Leave it, a parting gift if you will."

Liam responds, and none of us talk again.

I gather everything else we need, lock up the house, leaving our keys in the cabinet by the front door for the owners, along with an envelope with the next month's rent. I type an email to send them, letting them know we will be leaving.

The next thing I do is to change the license plates from the vans. I remove the old ones, switching them to the new ones. I take the remaining ones with my shovel, and I bury them next to where Mary's body is in the backyard. Dropping the shovel in the shed, I lock and bring the key to the cabinet with the rest.

"Boys time to go."

Nate announces from the driver's seat of the white van.

"On to the next."

Liam agrees and exits the driveway as I enter silently in the passenger seat next to my boyfriend. *This is for your own good Jess.*

A couple of hours pass and we park outside of a diner in hopes of getting some food. Liam is approaching right behind us and we pick a table far away, from any crowd to ensure some privacy.

"So, we are clearly not going to New York. Would you like to share with the group our next destination?"

I ask Nate once our food has arrived.

"We're going home."

He replies avoiding eye contact.

"Come again?"

Liam manages to say before I have even time to process what I just heard.

"You're joking right?"

I am joining in the confusion.

Nate chuckles.

"No, I am not. It is about time we go home don't you think? You got closure by killing Mary. We can travel from time to time to hunt, but we made some mistakes that can possibly pinpoint the last murders to us, by letting Jess in our lives, and then pissing her off by leaving her behind."

Liam turns to me.

"He is not exactly wrong." He points out.

I hate to admit.

"Yes he is not. Always the smart one isn't he? Home then."

I say and raise my glass to meet theirs.

Liam

We had been traveling for three days when we finally arrived in our hometown. We haven't been here since my family's death. Nate's parents were already thinking of moving to New York when we came to live with them.

They decided it was best for all of us if we moved and started over fresh. Too many rumors circulated in this town, and suspicion had risen about how both families died. Multiple tragic accidents were suspected to not be that much of an accident.

Nate's father knew the truth, though, and he still decided to adopt us. He knew everything. Mike told him what happened and the reasons behind, the first night we stayed at their house. He took pity on both of us and decided to protect us, and for that, we were always grateful.

The town seems so strange now, looking at it with different eyes and more information about our past. I know it is as much their fault as it is ours for what happened.

They knew about Mary. It is a small town; everyone knows everything. But none of them did anything to protect us when my sisters and I arrived at school with bruises. They did nothing to protect Mike when he shared his experience with the school psychologist the first year after his stepfather started coming to his room at night. He was told not to share the information with anyone else, just as I was told to hide the marks my father left on my body.

Now we are back here, and the memories of both good and bad come to mind as we park the vans in the driveway of Nate's family home. Our home. The only place we actually felt like we belonged for a moment or two.

I park and exit the car, tossing my keys to Mike.

"I am not dealing with the bikes right now."

I declare as I walk inside the house.

We all have our rooms still set up here, and I climb the long stairway to mine. Nate and Mike usually share one in every house we have lived in, but they both keep their things in separate rooms; in this house, their rooms are on the floor under mine.

I am more than grateful for that little detail, I don't need to be hearing sex noises all night and day. Without the hunts to keep them busy, I am sure they will do nothing else.

I step inside the dark room and turn the lights on. My eyes roam in the familiar space, a big bed in the middle with a Victorian-style bed frame. This house was inherited from son-to-son. Generations of Nate's family lived here and none of them ever thought to redecorate. The furniture is as old as the house, but in perfect shape and to my surprise I was always a fan of this room.

Dark red and black velvet fabrics, were used both for the bed's details and the curtains. The soft maroon carpet beneath my feet reminds me of a comforting memory of my first night in this room.

When we first arrived in the middle of the night to stay here, we were asked to pick a room. Mike had already been in their house countless of times, sneaking around with Nate. I knew that, but I wasn't supposed to, since none of them had admitted to themselves let alone to anyone else their sexuality.

With that information in mind, I picked the room at the top floor, next to Nate's parent's bedroom and left no choice to Mike but to choose the one next to their son's. Everyone was happy with that arrangement but of course, the boys picked up a fight about the room, just to hide their excitement of sharing the floor away from everyone else.

We had never come back here before, therefore the room arrangement never changed. Not that I will be willing to change it. We left Jess behind, I know that was the right decision, hell, I was the one who made it. That doesn't mean it is not hurting me as much.

For that reason, the comfort of this room will be much necessary as I lick my wounds and heal, while the boys heal theirs with sex and booze. I walk to the room next to mine, knowing there is a bar installed there fully stocked with Nate's father's whiskey collection. The man had a taste. We used to break into his alcohol stash, as college students and get drunk on an expensive bottle of whiskey every time we visited them in New York. He had a fully stocked bar there too.

Of course, the house is clean, and the mini-fridge is fully stocked with ice, even though we haven't been here in forever. We pay a lot of money to maintain the properties that originally belonged to Nate's family. It gives the pretend appearance that we are truly mourning the death of our parents by traveling the country, and eventually, we will return to live in one of the properties. The fact that we are here now solidifies this. It will work in our favor, especially after the mess we made in the last town.

We have trusted people who come here to air out the house, clean, and take care of the plants. Two days ago, Nate called them and asked them to fully stock the fridge, put ice in the mini-fridge of every room, and restock.

He also specified that any alcohol or any other items that had expired should be replaced. In addition, he asked them to redecorate both his room and Mike's with more modern aesthetic furniture. When I was asked about it, I refused to change anything in mine.

The rest of the house downstairs also remained as it was. It still surprised me how fast everything was done and ready, given the short two-day notice we provided and the demands of redecoration that came with it.

I pour some whiskey into my glass, raising it to no one but the ghosts of our past.

"To home."

I say and take a sip of my drink, settling into the armchair next to the bar.

Nate

Returning here brings out so many memories I have pushed away. Even though I had the perfect childhood and family, I have no bad memories exactly. The good ones haunt me as much as the bad ones would.

A sense of guilt of what I had become over the years of being away rushes through me as we step into the house.

Liam has already headed upstairs while we were taking out the suitcases from our van. We stored the bikes and van in the garage as soon as we finished.

After we took care of almost everything, Mike went to his bedroom to shower and rest.

I had to bring the last of our things inside, but now I crave a hot shower, a drink, and possibly some food from my favorite burger place. *God, I missed that place.*

I walk into my room, fully hoping to enjoy some moments of silence. I walk into the bathroom, turn on the shower, and I shed my clothes, dropping them on the floor. The moment my feet step into the shower, the bedroom door opens and Mike with a towel around his waist enters with a smirk on his face.

"Hey pup want to join me?" I ask and we both know that is exactly why he is here.

He doesn't say anything, just drops his towel next to my clothes and steps into the shower. I wrap one hand around his neck pulling him close as my lips crash to his, and our tongues play that sweet game of dominance swirling in a possessive kiss.

This man has always been the focus of my existence since we were kids, and he was a skinny fifteen-year-old getting into fights. Since I had to fight for him to stay alive. Since we didn't need blood or violence to be happy, just to survive.

He is everything I ever needed. Everything I will ever need. Everyone else is just noise when it comes to him. He is a priority. He is life. I love him with everything in me.

I know he has trouble expressing his feelings and I don't demand them but this kiss right now. This is everything I need him to say. Everything he needs to say. This kiss is like breathing air and watching the sunset. Happiness and hope all in one moment.

We both break our kiss and smile at the same time. I know he is thinking the same, I know him too well. We have been playing this game since we were teens, hiding from everyone.

I turn to the side and get the bottle of shampoo. I squeeze some on my hand.

"Turn around I want to wash your hair."

I would like nothing more than to fuck him right now, but at this moment after hours of traveling, and hundreds of emotions. Memories from our past, are hunting him for returning. I know he needs this more than sex. He needs to feel loved and I love taking care of him, as much as I enjoy every other moment with him.

He turns his back to me and leans backward letting me reach his hair. We are about the same height, but his posture gives me the right ankle to lather his hair with shampoo, and massage his scalp.

He moans in approval, putting a smile on my face. I am kissing his shoulder, and I grab the shower gel next. I clean him and he turns back to face me to return the favor. Even though this is not sex, and it is the simplest gesture of affection, it means more to me than anything else we have done.

Being back here, being like this, it makes me feel like I am seventeen again. Like the boy in front of me is the one who needs saving, and I am the one who will do anything and everything for him to survive.

When we have finished cleaning up, we both get dressed. Liam has now joined us in the living room, clearly not sober, but I ignore that. We decide to leave the house and walk to the burger place I love so much, hoping the food is still as good as it was when we used to live here.

Nothing has changed in this town, during the time we have been away. Everything is the same, and as we pass Mike's house, broken and abandoned still in his name. I see him pause; his eyes linger on the old house that is falling apart since he has done nothing to maintain it in the slightest. Both of them have ignored their family homes.

Liam's house is almost non-existent now; what remains of it after the fire stands two streets down the road from this one. This house, that once held every happy memory of Mike's childhood. The same house that was the foundation of his childhood terrors, is now decorated with graffiti calling him a murderer, since the rumors in this town are worse than the ghosts haunting it.

The forensic exam on his father's car showed that someone had tampered with the brakes. When the fire started in the middle of the night in Liam's house both boys barely made it out, while everyone else burned alive, rumors had it that Mike was responsible for both the car accident and the fire.

Of course, those rumors are indeed the ugly truth. The boys never intended for anyone other than Liam's father to die, but they were young and under the impression that they would have enough time to take everyone out once the fire started.

The house was mostly made of wood and was old; the flames took it so fast that they could barely escape themselves before they had to face the same fate as the rest.

My family took them in the same night. I already knew what was happening and woke up my father to take him to the station to help both of them with any accusations against their names. We already had a lawyer on standby, who was called immediately, and everyone was paid more than enough so that both boys walked out clean.

Liam,
The night of the fire

Mike is saying something I don't quite hear. Smoke is everywhere. The flames are growing so fast, I can't think. Screaming comes from the basement, and another person asks for help on the top floor. I am trying to get there but my feet are not moving.

I look back to the living room. My father's body on the floor is now burning, the smell of burning flesh haunts my nostrils. I try to shut down the knowledge that we did this. Mike killed him, and I helped him start the fire. Everyone will die here tonight. It is all our fault.

I think I am screaming or crying, then I realize it is not my voice. Someone is yelling at me. They shake my body. They pull me through the flames. I don't think I am moving but they keep pulling and yelling at me, and I am not sure what to do.

I realize that it is Mike, who is pulling me. He is now grabbing a chair, and throwing it at the window. The only window that is not wrapped in flames yet, and the glass shatters.

He tells me we need to move, we need to leave. I don't think I can. I can't leave them. This is all my fault. *I can't leave them, Mike. We can't leave them! You need to help them! Please help them!* I am screaming with all my strength but nothing comes out. He ignores me, and I am confused. He sure can't leave them to burn to death.

He pushes me through the window and I climb out. He is right behind me, pushing and pulling at my body forcing me to move. I think I am crying, but I don't feel tears leaving my eyes.

I am screaming in my head, and I am asking him to help them. I don't think he is listening to any of my pleas for help.

When we reach the road, I fall to my knees, as we watch the house burn to the ground. I hear sirens and police cars fill our street, voices are coming from everywhere. The screaming has stopped, but people are talking loudly. They will help them, I am sure of it.

I see them try to put out the fire, but no one is entering the house. *No, you need to help them; you don't understand, they are burning alive; you need to help them. They are innocent; please, help them!* I am pleading with them to help,but no one is listening to me.

They are questioning us; Mike is answering most of the questions. They are telling me that no one else made it out. They are explaining that my family is gone. They are asking more questions. How and why this happened. I am not sure if I am talking or not. I know Mike is, but I am not listening to what he has to say. *He let them burn.*

I don't know what to do so I stay silent, I try to listen if they are still crying or asking for help, but now everything is silent. The fire is coming down. The chatter from the firemen is calming down. Everything seems to be coming to an end. *They are gone. My mother is gone. My sisters are gone. This is all my fault.*

Liam,

Six months later...

I open my eyes with more effort than I should, feeling disoriented, my head is heavy and my stomach is turning upside down. I struggle to realize where I am, my eyes fall next to me on the two men I well recognized, both tied up, as I am myself.

"What the hell?!"

Mike's voice is heavy, as he comes out from his drug-induced nap. He struggles against the ropes but he quickly notices Nate still completely out of it, and he abandons his quest to get free.

"Nate are you okay?"

He calls and I see him pushing his body against Nate's in a failed attempt to wake him up.

"Liam what the fuck happened?"

He turns to me.

"She fucking drugged us."

I tell him. I recall the last thing I saw before face-planting that table, back in the bar we were having some drinks.

"Who did?"

He questions and I chuckle. *Who do you think Mike?*

"Jessica did."

I saw her talking to the waitress before she brought our drinks, and I would have said something, but I was really convinced it was my imagination. Nate is now coming out of his slumber granting and struggling against the rope around his hands and ankles.

"Let me guess. Jessica found us."

He points out and now I am laughing like a maniac. This small woman managed to take all of us out, somehow convinced someone to help her carry us to what seems like a van, and now taking us somewhere. Who knows where.

"That woman is crazy!"

Mike mumbles, pure irony coming from him, really, but it also could not be more true. The car stops suddenly and we all land against the door. Mike is now more pissed than ever and I hear steps surrounding the car.

"I guess, we will soon know what she wants."

Nate comments, he is being too calm for the situation. It is truly disturbing.

The door opens and a gun is pointed at us. She approaches with a knife cutting the rope around our legs and hands. Pulling each of us out, forcing us to stand. I look around realizing we are in a familiar maze. She brought us back to her town. *This is bad.*

Still holding the gun, she points to the maze and announces the rules that we all know too well.

"If you reach the scarecrow you are safe. If the sun comes up first, you may try another night."

Her voice reeks with authority. I am watching her carefully, she still has her gun pointed at us. She is dressed in all black and her hair is shorter. The curls giving her a innocent look, a vast contrast to her eyes full of rage and edgy clothes.

The woman I once fell for, with her bubbly personality and warm smile, who wore sundresses and had long curly hair and piercing blue eyes, is long gone. This woman in front of me is pissed, and we have to blame ourselves for it.

"Game on, boys."

She taunts, kicking Mike to the ground.

"Now run!"

A knowing look is exchanged between us, and we start running, all in different directions. I can tell Jessica is following me when her taunts start to be directed at me personally.

"Come on, Liam, you are not really running now, are you?"

She taunts, and I stop, hiding behind a stack of hay. *This is going terribly wrong.* I see the shadow of who I believe is Mike, running down the path that we both know leads to the scarecrow.

We all know this maze, like the back of our hands, but so does Jessica. If I learned anything about this woman, while I was stalking her, is how unpredictable she is. From fucking me in the back of the diner, she used to work at, to her being fucked by all three of us in a maze after running for her life. I don't think anything would scare her.

A gunshot echoes through the air, and Jessica's voice comes from the other side of the maze.

"Mike don't be naive you are not getting to the scarecrow."

Her laugh sounds twisted and evil. I can't tell if I am getting hard because of that, or being chased for my life does something to me. *Not now.* I try to silently command my dick to stand down.

"Liam?"

I hear a whisper behind me, and I turn to see both Mike and Nate hiding next to a nearby stack of hay. I crawl their way.

"What the hell is wrong with her?" Mike asks.

"Funny that it comes from you!"

Nate spits back before I could even say anything.

"We are all psychopaths; right now, her mental state is not our biggest concern." Nate explains.

"Fair."

I acknowledge, knowing well he does have a point. Every single one of us has done questionable things.

"You fucking left me."

Jessica's voice comes from the opposite side.

"For a valid reason, it seems."

Mike comments in a low voice, and both Nate and I burst into laughter, trying to keep it low.

"We need to figure out a plan." I state.

"She is clearly not going to let us reach the scarecrow, even if we do, I doubt she will let us go." Nate adds.

He has a point, she will never let us go. We wouldn't have let any women live that reached it either. Some of them did manage to get close, we always killed them at the end anyway.

"So what? Are we going to keep running in the hope that she stops being mad?"

Mike asks and I will give him that. This guy has a sense of humor even when he is being hunted by a crazy lady with a gun.

"Am I the only one getting hard by this?"

He questions again.

"Mike, stop thinking with your dick!"

Nate is pissed!

"Shut up! This is not the time to get horny."

I manage to say, a little too embarrassed to admit that I am as well.

Another gunshot echoes in the darkness of night, and I watch Mike patting himself to figure out if he was shot. Nate hits him in the back of his head.

"You were not shot. Stop it!" He tells him.

"We could beat her at her own game."

I finally say, both of them turn to look at me.

"She did beat the chase by fucking all three of us that night." I explain.

"Let's repay the favor." Nate agrees.

"Make her chase us, taunt her until she is a horny mess?" Mike finally gets the point.

" Exactly!"

Nate winks at him.

We go our separate ways again. I approach Jessica from behind still hiding behind the hay stacks. I see Nate in the other corner and Mike on the opposite side of him.

"Darling, are you sure you want to catch us?"

Nate talks from one side and Mike's voice comes next.

"We all know you don't have the guts to hurt us."

"If you wanted another good fuck, you could have asked, sweetheart."

I say from my side of the maze and we all start moving again.

"Yes angel, we would be happy to give you some dick, you didn't need to do all that." Mike taunts.

I see Jessica getting confused and horny while the table turns, and we are the ones hunting her again.

"Be a good girl and stop pretending you are not getting wet for us."

Nate's voice now comes from far away, and I watch her as she stops catching her breath.

I nod to Mike, and we both now running the opposite ways of her, she twirls in her spot trying to realize where the noise is coming from.

"Did you miss being on your knees for me?"

Mike asks her and I add .

"While I fuck that pussy making you moan and gasp around him?"

We are getting to her.

"You know I am the one with the gun this time, right?"

She asks but her voice reeks of desperation.

"How do you know we don't have hidden ones in the maze?"

Nate asks from behind me. I know what he is thinking. We have the knives we buried before leaving. But those are back in the house. Then my mind realizes. *I watched Mike throw his knife on the ground, when we chased Mary, after I stopped the game.*

I turn to Nate that now is standing directly behind me and whisper.

"The maze is abandoned. What are the chances Mike's knife is still here?"

He thinks for a moment.

"I am pretty sure I saw an object when we started running."

That could work.

"Mike, remember the time we chased Mary?"

I yell to my brother, and I hear him as he yells back.

"Oh, fuck yeah! Time to play angel!" he taunts her; his sinister laugh echoes in the maze as he runs.

I hear his steps fast approaching the entrance; Nate and Nate separate again, circling Jess. We need to confuse her enough for him to get to the knife. We only need one.

"So, what do you think, sweetheart?" I start. "Should we chase you instead? Remember the old days?"

She doesn't talk. I see her stop, mumbling something to herself; I am too far away to hear.

"I got it! Game on, slut!"

Mike yells from his side, and I smile to myself. *You are fucked now, Jess.*

"Darling, you can stop this before it's too late." Nate warns her.

I laugh because this woman is fucking Satan herself; she won't give up that easily. I am pretty sure she doesn't know we got the knife, though, or that it even exists. She is a smart girl; I am sure she checked the maze before we arrived, but if she had seen the knife, she would have picked it up and hidden it.

We are now coming from every side of her, and she points her gun at me and tries to search for Mike with her eyes.

"Stay back."

She tries to warn and I see Mike's inked hand wrapping around her stomach, his other hand holding the knife against her throat.

"Boo, bitch!"

His voice has a sinister tone, I have missed. He is back.

"Let me go."

She yells and thrusts against his hold trying to free herself. I close the space between us and I feel Nate's presence following me.

"Give me that."

I say as I take the gun from her, and toss it to Nate.

"Who has the power now little girl?"

Nate's voice sounds pissed. This man hates having no control of the situation. We all do. He does a terrible job handling it though. Mike gives me the knife and he wraps his hand that was holding it around her neck.

"Hold still!"

I order, but she still struggles against his hold. I can tell he is now choking her harder when she stops. I cut out her crop top first and her breasts burst out.

" No bra!" I announce.

"I knew you just wanted to get fucked baby girl!"

Nate is now provoking her.

Her skirt is next and as I cut it off her body, I see the lace thong she is wearing. I run my fingers on the fabric.

"Boys she is so wet for us." I tell them.

"Little Jess, you are soaked for us, aren't you?"

I tease, and I push the lace on the side, as I press two fingers inside her. She moans and her body reacts to me in an instant.

"So fucking tight."

I mumble mostly to myself, getting harder with every moment that passes.

"Did you miss us, Jess?"

I ask her and I remove my fingers from her pussy.

"Push her on her knees."

I order Mike this time. And he does as he is told. I free my cock from my jeans and I grab a handful of her hair, forcing her lips against it. She parts for me and I thrust in her mouth.

"Fuck Jess." I moan.

Both guys now are unzipping their pants as well. I let Nate pull her away from my cock, sweet Jess keeps her lips parted, and he pushes inside her mouth next. He is brutal, with every thrust making her choke around his cock and Mike is now kneeling on her level.

He fucks her with his fingers and she is practically riding his hand in a failed attempt to orgasm.

"Don't let her come!" I order. "Bad girls don't get rewarded!"

She tries to argue but Nate picks up his pace fucking her mouth harder.

"Push her on all fours!"

I order Mike and he is doing exactly what I asked. I take Nate's place and he is now behind her, pushing inside her with a hard thrust. Mike gets under her and starts eating her pussy as his boyfriend fucks her ass.

"Fuck you feel so good, Jess!" Nate praises her, and her moans are sending shots of electricity to my core.

"She is about to come, guys" Mike announces.

"Let her!"

I tell him. Her eyes close shut as she reaches her orgasm scared that I will take it away from her again. I am about to come myself and I pick up my pace, trying to raise her.

"I am close too."

I hear Nate announce and I can tell, from the way he is growling and moaning. He is filling her ass, as soon as his words come out of his mouth. My own orgasm is not far behind and I shoot cum down her throat as she moans around my dick swallowing every drop.

"Good girl."

Mike praises her before Nate hits her with the back of the gun, knocking her out. He picks her up to carry her to the van, and I search her skirt for a pocket that might contain the keys, but I come out empty.

"Boys, the keys were not on her."

I am looking around, to see if she dropped them.

"I saw them on the engine!"

Mike calls as he follows Nate. I pick up her ripped clothes and follow them.

"Where are we taking her?"

I am not willing to leave her behind again.

"Home!" Nate responds.

"You do not mean to tell me, we are going to drive with a naked woman in the back of a van, that doesn't belong to us now do you?"

He huffs. "Do you have a better idea?" He asks in return.

"We will stop at her house. I am sure she is still living there."

Even if she doesn't, she might have some clothes left there.

"We are going to take some clothes for her and head home."

We should have never left her. Everyone was under the impression we would ruin her, if we stayed. But she is as crazy as the rest of us and none of it is our responsibility. She was broken before we ever entered her life, Mike told me one night, the story she shared with him. We should have never left her behind.

Jessica

I open my eyes, feeling out of place. Everything is dark, my body is sore, and my head is killing me. My body rocks against something, and I feel the floor with my fingers. I am in the back of the van I used to kidnap the guys, the realization hits me.

"Welcome back sweetheart!" someone tells me.

"How was your nap?"

I recognize the voice. It is Liam but I can't see him. I try to move my hands and legs but I can't. *The bastards tied me up again.*

"Liam let me go!"

I yell and I hear Mike's laugh from the same direction. The voices come from the driver's seat, that must mean Nate is in the back with me. It doesn't take more than a second before Nate's voice shutters that idea.

"Darling, how is your head?" He is also in the front.

"Ask her how that pussy feels instead."

Someone else talks, I am pretty sure that was Mike.

The sarcasm is a clear indication of his psychotic ass. I try to set myself free but I can't.

I relax against the rope instead, and decide to play it smart. *They have kidnapped me before, they didn't kill me then, they won't kill me now.*

"Where are we going?"

I need clues.

"Home."

Home? Where is home, Liam? Like he read my thoughts, Nate answers.

"We should have never left you behind, Jess"

That's right, you shouldn't have!

"We are going to make it up to you."

Sure you will Mike.

"Are you going to make it up to me by kidnapping me?"

I sass him, and this time Liam responds. I am getting pretty good at telling them apart.

"It is just for your safety."

He laughs and adds.

"We thought you might try to jump out of the van." *He is not wrong.*

"At least you dressed me up this time."

I notice, running my fingertips the best I can against my body. *I am not naked. That's a good sign.*

"As much as I would love to have you naked all the time Jessica, we couldn't drive with you naked for three days." Nate informs me.

Okay, that is a good clue. Where would we go that we would need to drive for three days, away from my town? Fuck Jess, why didn't you stick with school and geography.

"If you promise to not make a run for it, we can take a break and cut you loose." *That was Liam.*

Before I can answer, Mike's voice comes again.

"I say we leave her like that until we arrive." *Don't be a dick, Mike.*

"She needs to be punished for kidnapping us." *Seriously? You kidnapped me first!*

"You are not wrong."

Nate acknowledges. A pause follows and he speaks again .

"Tell me, darling, how did you find us?" He questions.

"Mike told me about your favorite bar in New York when we were talking about moving there. I moved to the city right after you left me. I tried to find you. Then I realized you never got there. So, I started hanging out at that bar. I started working there and made friends with the owner and the staff. They were the ones who helped me put you in the van when you finally decided to come visit." I explain my plan.

"Smart girl."

A hint of admiration in Nate's voice; he is proud of me.

"You know, we decided to leave you behind only with your benefit in mind."

You could have asked Liam.

"We are truly sorry for our decision; however, we need to start working on our communication. We can't keep kidnapping each other to prove a point."

Nate adds and the other two laugh.

"Fair point."

I agree. He is not wrong. I fell in love with all three of them, and I never fell out of love in the six months we have been apart. From how things progressed in the maze, I can say they haven't either.

Jessica

I wished for them to come back countless times in those six months. I waited for a month before I moved to New York on my own. I took every dollar I had saved. Since my father was back at work and doing well, I had nothing to keep me home.

He did not need me anymore, and I for sure didn't want to keep living with ghosts. My mother's image haunts that house, and my brother's cry still echoes in my ears every night, years later. I tried so hard for that baby to survive and even though I know I would have failed either way, I could never keep myself from feeling guilty about it.

The boys were the closest to happiness I ever got. And they left me. They saw me, the real me, and they ran away. *Not even serial killers want you, Jess.* That little voice tells me again it is sad how much I believe it.

They didn't want to stay with me. I wasn't good enough for them. Oh well, this is not their choice to make. I am done being ignored and my failed attempt to hunt them in the maze was my way of telling them. No man will leave me behind again. Especially not those deranged assholes. They are stuck with me.

The car stops and someone opens the door. Liam pulls my blindfold and cuts off the rope around my limbs. They are not planning to keep me hostage, which is a good sign.

"Behave sweetheart."

Nate warns and I nod.

I look down, at the clothes I am wearing. I recognize the ones, I left on my bed in case I need to change after the hunt. I also notice next to me the two bags I had left in my room. They are actually bringing me with them this time.

I had a plan when I left. Get to New York, find them, and bring them back in the maze to teach them a lesson. *Letting them fuck me, was not part of the plan.*

One could argue I was the one to learn that lesson instead of them, but I am not regretting it. They are back, and this time they took me with them. *Progress Jess, this is progress.*

As we walk towards the restaurant on the side of the road, the smell of burned bacon hits my nostrils, and I salivate at the thought of it. I am starving. I am not sure when was the last time, I had anything to eat. As a statement, my stomach growls and Mike laughs.

When I turn to face him he smirks and wraps his arm around me. It is almost like they never left. Like the last six months of misery and loneliness never existed.

"Let's sit in the back. "

Liam announces as he walks inside to find a table. He is avoiding to look me in the eyes. I realize he was probably the one to decide to leave me behind. Guilt washes over him like a wave, this man doesn't seem to handle emotions well at all.

They all take a seat at the round table and Mike pulls me, to take the one next to him. He is being clingy and that makes me feel so loved and wanted. It fills my heart with warmth.

The waitress approaches our table to take the order, and Nate takes charge of ordering for everyone, Reminding me of the time we went to Rosa's Diner, and I did the same, wanting them to try all my favorite things off the menu.

"We are sorry for leaving you behind, Jessica."

Liam is still avoiding looking at me, but his voice sounds sincere.

"I understand."

I want to make sure he knows I am not holding a grudge about it. I only wanted them to love me and accept me. I was never truly mad at them, only hurt.

Mike

Jessica is sitting next to me, she is smiling and talking like nothing happened. This woman is a fucking goddess with hellfire inside her. My brother is finally smiling again. Nate is looking less mad than usual, and I feel like my family is complete again.

Liam has been sobbing in private for months now. We returned home and never went hunting in the duration of the six months away from her. I tried to recommend that we do it a couple of times, Nate did too. But Liam spent his waking hours with a glass full of whiskey and ice, looking through the window of the master bedroom.

That bedroom once belonged to Nate's parents, he has refused to enter it since their death. Liam kept hiding there, avoiding Nate. I visited from time to time, to give him some food, that he mostly refused.

He has lost a lot of weight and you can tell, how the once fit man, is turning skinny now. His eyes have bags under them and his skin is so pale you would think, the sun hasn't looked at this guy for at least six months. It would be completely true though. He didn't leave once after the first night we went out for dinner.

I caught a glimpse of him crying once or twice. He is now smiling and looking at her, the same way he did when he would spend his hours watching her work. He used to observe her with such lust in his eyes, it was the one thing I noticed, when we were stalking him. He always seemed like his heart was aching for this woman, I am pretty sure it was.

I believe he fell for her way before they even got together. I think he fell for her the day, he saw her for the first time. Only that would explain, why he was so willing to risk everything for her. It would explain why he couldn't stay away, even when he figured out we were on to him.

Liam wears his emotions like a badge. Even when he bottles them you can see, what he is feeling. He feels everything, and I always envied that about him. I always wanted to be more like him, but something broke inside me when I was eight and I never got it back together fully.

I brush with my fingers Nate's thigh and he smiles at me. We don't need to talk about it, we both know we should have gotten her back months ago. *She belongs with us.*

Jessica,

Three days later...

We had to stop a couple of times but we have finally arrived to our destination.

I get out of the passenger's seat, that I spent the last four hours on Mike's lap. The house in front of me looks like a mansion.

Big windows across its walls, the paint looks like it is fresh, and a lady opens the door wearing some type of uniform. I suppose, she is some sort of maid for the guys. Dog runs out of the door and greets me.

I pet him and scratch his ear.

"I missed you too buddy."

Nate is talking to the woman and Liam is carrying my bags inside. Their own things have been shipped from the hotel in New York two days ago. I listened to Nate, when he was arranging this on the phone the first night in one of our stops.

I stay still in the same spot. The door of the van has closed behind me and Mike is standing next to me. I don't know what to do, I don't feel like I belong here, until he leans in and whispers in my ear.

"Welcome home Jess."

He smiles, and he joins the rest of them. I stay put, watching the three men I fell in love with being happy, for the first time since I met them. *We are finally home.*